THE
Opoponax

THE
Opoponax
MONIQUE WITTIG

Translated by Helen Weaver

DAUGHTERS, INC.

Plainfield, Vermont

Daughters, Inc., First Printing 1976

ISBN: 0-913780-15-4
Library of Congress Catalog Card Number: 76-7818

Manufactured in the United States of America

THE
Opoponax

The little boy whose name is Robert Payen comes into the classroom last, crying, Who wants to see my weewee-er? Who wants to see my weewee-er? He is buttoning his pants. He has beige wool socks on. Sister says to be quiet, and why is he always the last to arrive. This little boy who only has to cross the street and is always the last to arrive. You can see his house from the door to the school, there are trees in front of it. Sometimes during play period his mother calls him. She is at the top window, you can see her above the trees. Sheets are hanging out the window.

Robert, come and get your muffler. She yells in a loud voice so that everyone can hear, but Robert Payen does not answer, so that everyone goes on hearing the voice that calls his name. The first time Catherine Legrand came to school she saw the playground from the road, the grass and the lilacs by the fence. The fence is made of shiny metal wire in the shape of diamonds, when it rains the drops run down and stick in the corners, it is over her head. She holds her mother's hand and her mother pushes open the door to the school. There are lots of children playing in the playground but not a single grownup except for Catherine Legrand's mother and it would be better if she did not come again, school is only for children, she'd better tell her, should she tell her? Inside the school is very big, there are lots of desks, there is a big pot-bellied stove with more of the diamond-shaped fencing around it, you can see the chimney which goes almost to the ceiling, it is pleated in places, Sister is standing on a ladder by the window, she is doing something, she is trying to close the top window. When Catherine Legrand's mother says Good morning Sister, Sister gets down and takes the little girl by the hand and tells her mother to leave while nobody is looking, everything will be fine. Catherine Legrand hears the noise coming from the playground, why don't they let her be with the other children, maybe it is because she is not really in school yet, because if this is school it's not the way she imagined it. It looks just like her house only bigger. Sometimes in the afternoon the children are supposed to sleep but it's only pretend. You cross your arms and put them on the table and put your head on top of them. You close your eyes. You're not allowed to talk. Catherine Legrand opens one eye every once in a while but that's not allowed either. You sing rounds, At my right hand is a rose tree which will bloom in the month of May, and you hold out your right hand. Catherine Legrand looks to the right, it is not May so the rose tree has not bloomed yet. And you have tea. Everyone has a lunch basket and at four o'clock Sister picks up all the baskets and calls, Whose basket is this? and you say Mine if it's yours. Inside is a piece of bread, a chocolate bar and an apple or an orange. Catherine Legrand always eats hers on the way to school although she has been told not to but she can't help herself. Sometimes she just takes a few bites, and then Sister says, Whose basket is this with the half-eaten apple? Often she tries not to remember whether or not she has eaten the apple or orange before time for tea so she will be surprised or on the chance that the apple will become whole again if she really does forget. Catherine Legrand cheats, she knows very well that it won't work because she never manages to forget completely and she is only a tiny bit surprised when she is handed her basket without an apple or with an apple which is not much more than a core, and in any case she will never be able to forget what is in her basket. Sister peels the oranges. With her knife she cuts off the rind in a

7

circle and it comes off the fruit in curls. When she is through she hangs the longest curls, the ones she managed to keep whole without breaking them, on the door, they hang all the way down the door, and they turn when you touch them, Sister won't give them away. The little fat girl whose name is Brigitte because she is fat grabs Catherine Legrand by the neck, Catherine Legrand smiles at her, the little girl's cheeks spread apart and go back beside her mouth immediately, she pulls Catherine Legrand by the neck, she turns red, then she leans on Catherine Legrand's neck and bends down to the ground still pulling, Catherine Legrand falls flat on her face and gets up. The little fat girl whose name is Brigitte comes back, Catherine Legrand does not smile, this time she is ready, she pulls again, her cheeks spread and swell, her head is very near, her hair is gray, when she pulls she is strong, you're flat on your face in no time and if you cry it runs down the crack in the floor. You mustn't get up or it will begin again. The class repeats after Sister, sixty-eight, sixty-nine. They are counting. Seventy-one, seventy-two. Sister is Belgian. They go back to one: one, two, three. They play Cat in the Grass. You have to run fast and find something to sit on. If you are too tired you say Thumbs and hold up your thumb. Catherine Legrand sits on the fence. Her panties tear on a nail. Rip! Catherine Legrand gets down and runs carefully, yelling Thumbs. Oh dear! Nobody has seen anything, but she can't keep on playing without panties even if the others don't know. Catherine Legrand hangs around Sister without saying anything. It's like when she dreams she is in the street in her nightgown or even naked because she has forgotten to get dressed. She says Thumbs when someone comes near. Sister takes off her panties and mends them. Catherine Legrand watches her without moving. Down below the children are still running. The little girl whose name is Jacqueline Marchand calls Thumbs and puts up her thumb. It is raining. You are playing in the classroom. You are holding the hands of the little boy whose name is Guy Romain and who sits next to you. You straddle the bench and sing *Maman les petits bateaux qui vont sur l'eau*, bending together to make a boat. This is how you fail to notice Sister who has just given the signal for the end of play period and you receive a slap on both cheeks, it rings in your ears and makes your head spin. It is boring when there isn't any school. Catherine Legrand walks around in the garden. She goes to the gate and watches the people go by on the road. Only a few people go by and none of them are children. You can see some peach pits and plum pits in the gutter. You can slip out of the garden secretly and walk down the road a little way. You walk at the edge of the pavement near the curb, not stepping on the cracks between the curbstones. You step over the curb. You are back before anyone has noticed. The sky is gray. It looks like rain, or as if the sun is about to come out. This weather has a funny smell, as if there were damp grass in the sky that you can't see. Maybe the sun is about to come out from behind those lighter clouds. Catherine Legrand walks with her eyes closed, pressing her hands against her eyelids so she won't be tempted to look. She gives herself time to come back up the path walking very slowly, to do this she takes steps no longer than her shoes. The idea is to put your left foot in front of your right foot very carefully, so that the heel of the left shoe touches the toe of the right one. She will open her eyes a crack and look down at the ground to see where she is, but only a crack. When she has reached the end of the path she will start all over again walking the other way, with her eyes still closed the whole time, then back up the path again one more time, meanwhile repeating Sun, sun, every time she takes a step. When she has finished she will let herself take her hands away from her face, and maybe the sun will show behind the clouds. The family is at table. They are talking about grandpa's stroke, he can't move his right side, even his right eye is closed, his mouth is pulled down at the corner. Father and Mother look at Catherine Legrand. She is not supposed to talk. Her right side slides down the chair, pulling her down, Catherine Legrand follows it down, they see her between the chair and the floor, she stays there wedged, Catherine Legrand can't go either way, she is looking at the floor, she is jerking back and forth like a mechanical toy. Catherine Legrand has been attacked. The thing climbed up her chair while they were eating and not watching and now it has jumped on her, right under her father's and mother's noses. They look at her without moving. They can't help her. She must fight it herself. Catherine Legrand tries to get out a few words, her efforts are terrible, and before she knows it they come out as screams. The garden is full of water. You can see the branches of the tree through the window when you are sick in bed. There are two pillows under your head so you can be sitting up and lying down at the same time. Mother says, look at the bullfinch, Where mama, show me where. Right there, on the fork of the cherry tree. Catherine Legrand sits up. Down below the ground is all black and covered with petals that have fallen off the cherry tree. The flowers broke last night, mama. The tall little girl whose name is Inès calls for Catherine Legrand to take her to school. She has some other children with her. Mother calls her the little girl from town. You walk along the national highway, you cross it when you come to the supermarket. Inès says, That is where my mother does her shopping. You are on a road. There are lilac leaves and red dahlias against the high diamond-shaped fencing. In the meadow by the shed Monsieur Magnier's mare is standing with her head down. She begins to run along the wall as fast as she can. There are covered paths where people go by on bicycles. In the winter you wear wool socks. Your thighs are red and chapped from the wind. You play in a ring in the covered playground with Sister. You ask Sister, Where is your husband? She says, Up above, pointing

to the sky. You look at the sky. You don't see anything. You tell Sister, You can't see your husband.
Sister doesn't want to answer. When you insist she
says that she is not really surprised, there are too many
clouds. He is sitting behind them in an armchair.
Maybe he will come home at noon with the paper.
You say to Sister, When will he come? He is not
coming. But when? Never. Then is he dead? No he
is not dead. And where do they put dead people? In
a hole. But do they go to heaven? *There was a little
boat that had never been to sea.* You go for a walk.
You do not wear your smocks. You keep your coats
and mufflers on. Sister carries a big basket with all the
lunch baskets inside. You sit down on the grass. You
play with pebbles, how many pebbles am I holding
in my hand. Sister asks riddles. My first is a metal, my
second has wings, my third is found in the fields and
the whole thing is a crayon. The little boy whose
name is Alain Trévise and who lives next door has
picture books. There are totems in them. A totem is
red yellow blue animals which are stuck on top of
each other and stay that way forever. It looks like a
red yellow blue pole but it is not a pole because it
flies. When Catherine Legrand comes home from
school in the evening she is afraid of being attacked
by totems. The tall little girl whose name is Inès says,
You're silly, they don't fly at that time of day, Well
when do they fly? I have never seen them fly and
maybe they don't fly in this kind of a country. What
is a country? It is where you are. Then where you

aren't is not a country? No. Well then, there aren't
any totems where you aren't if it's not a country, are
there? I don't know. Well then, where you are is a
country and there are totems. Yes but they won't
hurt you when I am with you. Catherine Legrand
holds onto the hand of the tall little girl whose name
is Inès because you never know what might happen
and if they have to run Catherine Legrand is not good
at it, she is always behind. When you go into the
meadow you are very careful not to talk loudly. You
crawl under the barbed-wire fence on your stomach
but it's not allowed. You might be sued. So as not to
be seen you go and hide in the hay which is gathered
into a heap in the middle of the field. You are with
the tall little girl whose name is Inès and the boy
whose name is Alain Trévise. You play to see who is
touching the hand of the person inside the haystack.
The little boy whose name is Alain Trévise wriggles.
Someone touched something else of his. You haven't
finished the game when Inès runs out of the haystack.
You hear a voice shouting Hounds of hell, hounds of
hell. You start running in all directions. Catherine
Legrand is behind and cries as she runs, falling down
and getting up again, she can't catch up with the
others. Why are they running away so fast, what are
hounds of hell, that means the devil is there, they are
the devil's dogs, yes the devil likes to kidnap children,
but why does he like to kidnap children? They haven't
done anything wrong. The whole length of the field
is between Catherine Legrand and the others. Cath-

erine Legrand falls onto the stubble. It prickles. When Catherine Legrand turns around she can't see the hound of hell. How big is he? Maybe he is a dog that you can't see or maybe you have to wait until you are as old as Inès to be able to recognize him, maybe it is when there is a flower in the hay, a poppy or a cornflower or maybe a piece of wood, you must start running again, maybe the dog is already there all around because you can't see him, maybe you will never be able to run again, anyway it's serious if a big girl like Inès is afraid. You are reading whole sentences out loud. The miller's wife mills the corn. The miller leads the sheep. The sheep eats the corn of the miller's wife. In the reader there is a sheep which is bigger than the miller's wife. There are white balls all around him, they are wool. Liliane does the laundry. You repeat after Sister. Liliane does the laundry. Sister copies what it says in the book on the blackboard. She points to each syllable with the big wooden ruler. When Sister hears something that is not right, she taps the blackboard and says, Again, tapping the syllable, *laun*, *laun*, again, *laun*. Catherine Legrand has snow boots. When it is raining or snowing, Sister puts them in front of the stove to dry with the shoes and other snow boots. Catherine Legrand can't fasten them by herself. They have buttons on the side. Sister forgets to button them. It's hard to walk. Catherine Legrand comes home from school with her snow boots open. They gape at the sides. It is harder and harder for Catherine Legrand to put one foot in front of the other. Something heavy has come in through the opening and Catherine Legrand simply can't lift her foot. She looks behind her. There is a cloud which is coming lower and lower. In it there is a little old man who is laughing. Catherine Legrand wants to bend over and fasten her snow boots, she can't, she wants to run, she can't because of all the weight that has come in. When she turns around the little old man has almost caught up with her, you can see his mouth plain as day, he is chuckling, you can hear him, he is going hee hee in the back of his throat. Catherine Legrand makes a heroic effort to lift her feet off the ground. She is barely able to do it and each time she does, she is pulled to the side, first to the right side, then to the left side, this is why she doesn't make any progress, she just goes one, two, right, left, like a metronome, she absolutely must move, leave this place, get out of here, it's almost dark, the little old man is right behind, hee hee hee. Catherine Legrand makes a superhuman effort and it comes out a scream. The little Jesus who goes to school, you give him candies, a red apple to put in his mouth, a bouquet of flowers to place on his heart. You are learning to say his prayer and you even go to mass on Sunday. You have a book with pictures on the pages and other pictures that aren't on the pages. When you drop them you can't put them back into the book right because of your woolen gloves and when you take the gloves off by pulling with your teeth you can't get your fingers back into the fingers of the gloves. You are with other children. You are kneeling on wooden benches. Sometimes you are allowed to sit down. There is a dent in your knee in the place where it presses against the bench. You run your finger over it for fun. It is all white because it's cold. You draw with crayons. A house with a pointed roof. You make the shutters green. It is surrounded by flying birds from top to bottom. You make the wings blue, but you can't see their beaks. You can't see their eyes either. There are children who draw birds from the side so you can see their eyes. The mother is hanging out the wash in the garden. You make the mother. She lifts her arms. On each side of her you can see the wash which she has already hung out in squares. Catherine Legrand wears panties that stick to her legs when it is cold. They bother her when she walks she feels them everywhere she has two legs yes and between her legs the seam makes it hard to walk. You don't wear panties when you're little. You don't like them because they divide you in two, Catherine Legrand but also what is in the panties which is not exactly Catherine Legrand. Perhaps Catherine Legrand is the only little girl who wears panties and who is not exactly a little girl. In the playground several children are squatting together making weewee. The little boy whose name is Robert Payen says, Look at my weewee-er. Why do you have that? Because I am a big boy. Will I have one too? Yes when you are big like me. The little boy with the weewee-er whose name is Robert Payen is sick. He has enormous mufflers. His eyes glitter, he is very white. Sister says he will not come to school. Sister says he will not come to school any more. Sister says he is dead. The shutters of the house that shows above the trees are closed. After class the tall little girl whose name is Inès takes the children over to the house. Maybe you will be able to see something. The house is all closed up you can't see anything. The little girl whose name is Pascale Delaroche nudges another little girl with her elbow, Understand? The other little girl whose name is Françoise Pommier says, Oh. Her mouth is very round. You don't understand anything. You walk around the house by the highway. In the garden a truck without any wheels is half buried in the ground. In back of the house the shutters are closed except on the ground floor where the window is open. You can see a family at table. There is a plate in front of each person. The seated children seem very grownup. You can't hear any talking. The father gets up and closes the window. He pushes back his chair and speaks in a very loud voice. You can't understand what he says. The windowpanes tremble when he slams the window shut. He seems angry. You run away. The children are whispering something to each other. The one who is talking stands on tiptoe to reach the ear of the one who is listening, and who is taller. Catherine Legrand says, Are children put in a hole too when they are dead? No one knows. All along the road you must look out for sewer holes. You decide that you'd better not walk too close to them because now you know

that this is where they put dead people and maybe
dead children too. They open up under the pavement
you can't see them from a distance you must look
carefully to see they are there, they open up on the
street if you slip and fall into them you are dead.
Sewers are there to suck things in, they can kill you.
You can die first of course and that is where you go
anyway. But if you are sucked in by accident you die
too and besides nobody knows you're dead. It is not
unheard of, children dying before their fathers and
mothers. When you hear children playing outside you
can't fall asleep. The sheets are hot you're uncomfort-
able, you wish you were dressed so you could run
outside. It is still light the windows are open. Smells
of dried grass, of trees which were warm all day and
which stir in the wind come through the blinds. Someone is watering the garden. You can hear the soft hissing noise of the stream of water. The ground has also
been hot and now it gives off a smell from the water
which is poured onto it. The children are running on
the road. They are yelling because they are happy. It
sounds like swallows crying only every once in a
while there are louder cries which you recognize as
the cries of a child who has come near or who is lost
in the game. Other cries answer him. They overlap,
meet, one outlasts another by an instant, you can't
tell the voices apart when you are lying in bed and
it's time to go to sleep. The slats of the blinds make
very long shadows across the ceiling. Sometimes the
shadows swell and go from one side of the ceiling to

the other. They don't stop moving and when you close your eyes there are red and green ones between your eyelids and your eyes. Sometimes there are yellow stripes across them. They are always changing shape you don't have time to keep up with them. Mother says there is down in the pillow. It moves against your ears, it makes a sound like dry leaves and keeps you awake. There is also something at the bottom of the pillow which makes the same sound as a drum but which is very far away, it is a beating sound, it echoes in your head. You can look over the wall and see the town children playing. You jump up and grab the top of the wall with your hands. After that all you have to do is scrabble up with your shoes until you are on top. You see some little houses all in a row. In front of a door a mother is shaking the mat you wipe your feet on. She puts it on the ground and kicks it with her feet one after the other. She turns it over and does the same thing again. When she picks it up there is a pile of dust on the ground in the shape of the mat. She sweeps the dust with a broom. The children are far away. They are running around the houses. As they turn the corners their feet skid on the coal dust of which the road is made. You throw stones at them so they will look toward the wall. You don't hit them. You throw the stones against a door and you must climb back down the wall as fast as you can, letting your knees hang against the wall so you can find the ground with your toes. You are playing. You are putting spiders in a box. You pull off all their legs so they can't escape while the lid is off. You leave the little hooks they have in front. They use these to get around. You put them on the cement and make them run races. You put them in houses. You throw them out. In the schoolyard you are playing doctor. Sister is sitting in a chair. The doctor uses lilac leaves for a compress. He applies lilacs dipped in mud to the arms, the thighs, and the stomach. You read whole sentences. Sister writes them on the blackboard. The weaver weaves the wool. The tiles on the roof will last all summer. She points to each syllable with the tip of the wooden ruler. Sister says, Repeat after me, The tiles on the roof. You repeat the same sentence over and over. You are on the bench. You're not allowed to move. You sink way down in your seat. Sister asks the little boy whose name is Pierre Bertrand to read the sentence by himself while she follows with the ruler on the blackboard. Pierre Bertrand does not understand what Sister tells him. He does not read. He does not open his mouth. He stands in the aisle. Sister puts him on a bench by himself. She says, We will repeat again for Pierre Bertrand, The tiles on the roof. When you are grownup you will be able to read from a book without the ruler and without Sister all by yourself without repeating. You will read pages and pages without stopping. Do you love your mother? The little girl whose name is Josiane Fourmont says this. I love my mother, yes I love my mother. How much do you love her? This much. You hold out your hands to show how much. Catherine Legrand holds her hands as far apart as she can. And you? This much. The fingers of the little girl whose name is Josiane Fourmont are almost touching. What's that, you don't love your mother? Not very much. Sister jumps down from the platform. Her habit flies straight out behind her. She crosses the room in two strides. Sister pulls Josiane Fourmont by the ear and forces her to her feet away from the bench, Sister's hand keeps shaking her ear. When she is through the ear stands away from the head all purple and bruised. In the playground the little boy whose name is Guy Romain is playing car. He runs a little way, stamping his feet on the ground. He moves his hands in a circle in front of his stomach. They turn around from front to back. He is in reverse. He is going forward though. The little girl whose name is Pascale Delaroche yells, Not like that when you're going forward. Guy Romain doesn't listen. His mouth is making a monotonous sound. Pascale Delaroche shows him the right way to turn your hands, from back to front. She says, That's how you go forward. Pascale Delaroche goes up to the little boy whose name is Guy Romain and pulls his hands so he will turn them the right way. Guy Romain pulls away from her still making the sound with his mouth and still stamping his feet on the ground. He makes his turn leaning as far as he can to the right when he reaches the wall. He straightens up again before coming to the school.

You are hiding behind the lilacs. You hear voices yelling somewhere, You're it. The leaves are wet from the rain. They are spaced very evenly along the branches. On each one they are arranged symmetrically on both sides, they look the same, except at the end where a larger leaf weighs down the whole branch. A bird sits in the big fork of the lilac tree. He won't fly away if you don't move. The ground is a glowing brown, soaking wet, very shiny. You are squatting. Sometimes one foot slips out from under you and you have to put it back under your thighs. You put your hand on the ground to steady yourself. The bird begins to sing. On the other side of the wire fence is the road, another wire fence and behind the second wire fence the meadow with the shed. You can see the roof rising behind the lilac trees. You can hear voices jumbled together. I saw you. It's your turn. No fair looking through your hands. Turn your face to the wall. You wait a little longer. Someone must already have turned his face to the wall, because there is silence. The bird flies away. Mademoiselle is having a conversation with a lady at the door of the classroom. The children are talking very loud. They are laughing. They are roughhousing. They are throwing erasers. Hélène Corte runs across the room. There is a blackboard that runs the whole length of the wall. Mademoiselle turns around and says, Be quiet. She smiles at the lady. You can see that they are returning to the subject they are discussing. Now you can't see anything but the lady's hat. Mademoiselle is in the way. You have a notebook on your desk. You write in it with a black pencil. Mademoiselle writes the date in ink at the top of the page every day. You press on the paper to form the letters. You even make holes. You play boat with Alain Trévise. Alain Trévise's mother comes in every once in a while to see what the class is doing, you pretend to look in your books. Alain Trévise's mother is very tall, she has a lot of very white hair that sticks out all over her head. She talks in a loud voice. She says, You are the devil. Alain Trévise gets slapped and runs around the table. So does his mother. You put the ninepins on the floor. On top of the ninepins you put the blackboard. When you sit on it it rolls backward. Alain Trévise says, We're pitching, put up the sails. You make the boat go by wiggling. The black smock is smudged with chalk from the blackboard you are sitting on. Alain Trévise whistles the captain's orders with the whistle. A short whistle blast. A long whistle blast. Alain Trévise's mother comes into the room. You are attacking the battleship, the overturned armchair. Alain Trévise yells, They surrender. Anyway the ship is gone. The blackboard is standing up, so is the armchair, the ninepins are in the toy chest. Catherine Legrand can't write. She presses on the paper with the black pencil. She makes letters that stick out on both sides beyond the two lines you are supposed to write inside of, they stick out above and below, they touch the other lines, they are not straight. Mademoiselle says, Begin again. First you make d's and a's, then r's. The bellies of the s's are always too big, the r's fall forward on their canes. The lady who lives on the top floor of the house has a little voice when she talks to Catherine Legrand. She takes her into her garden. You begin to pick peas. They are hanging from sticks in a row. Some are at the very top, but most are in the middle. Many have fallen to the ground and scattered. You go and hunt for them under the leaves. You pull on the pod and the stalk breaks. If you don't do it right the whole thing comes out, the whole stalk comes away from the bottom, you have pea tendrils around your wrists from pulling and the peas come out the top of the pod when you crush it with your fingers. You put them in the lady's market bag. There are late pea plants which are still all in bloom. Some have flowers and pods at the same time. The lady leans over without squatting down. She has a flat bun on her neck. She is a much older lady than Catherine Legrand's mother. She talks all the time. Sometimes she stops and looks as if she is about to cry. Her nose wrinkles. You don't know what it's like, you're too little. The trouble I have with that man! I know he's sick but even so. Last night he yelled because the soup was scalding hot, scalding he said I'm going to throw it in your face you do it on purpose, on purpose, me, on purpose, me. He has a tapeworm. He eats but he gets thinner. The lady has a funny smell. Like apples rotting under the tree. Her cheeks were soft the time Catherine Legrand kissed her. You follow her. You listen to her. You pick peas. Some have beetle holes with something that looks like a string of tiny beads coming out of them. There is something tickling you behind the knees, when the lady stops talking you become very weak, you feel as if you are about to fall down. And then meat is expensive, bread is expensive, milk is expensive, eggs are expensive, shoes are expensive, living is expensive. Mademoiselle says, Catherine Legrand, your notebook is not up to date. You must make up the writing lessons for Monday, Tuesday, Wednesday, Friday, and Saturday, the others are doing another Monday's. Between Catherine Legrand's notebook and those of the rest of the class there are three Mondays. Pages of m's, l's, and b's with vowels. Pages of houses, stones, pictures, fountains, avenues, pages of lions eating lambs, of Leon learning his lesson, of Jeanne washing her hands. The pencil is too sharp it makes holes in the paper. The pencil is too blunt it makes thick letters. The eraser doesn't erase. It makes what is already there and what you want to take away bigger. Mademoiselle says bad workers always have bad tools. Mademoiselle writes the date in ink at the top of the pages that must be filled. Catherine Legrand is alone on the bench, alone in the row, alone against the wall. The wall has a window which is almost as high as the ceiling. You can't see anything but sky. It is on the side of the meadow with the shed. When it is warm Mademoiselle lowers the wooden blind and the yellow slats it is made of cast long rectangular shadows inside the classroom. Mademoiselle is at the door of the classroom with Dominique Baume's father. She is shaking her head from right to left and laughing. She has glasses on. All you can see is her black back and her black legs. Through the open door you look at the covered playground. The roof comes down low it is dark under it even in the afternoon. The stove is small and round. The fire screen is made of little pieces of metal. When it is cold out they get red from the heat given off by the stove. You warm round stones on top of the stove and pick them up. You wait until they are burning hot. Even with your woolen gloves on, you can hardly hold them. You shift them from one hand to the other. You drop them on the floor. You feel them from time to time. You pick them up again. When they are warm you slip them against your palm inside the glove, which you stretch to make room for them. You covet a stone that is more polished, rounder, and bigger and belongs to someone else. As soon as they cool off you put them back on top of the stove. You are picking buttercups and dandelions. The hollow stems contain a liquid that leaves brownish stains on your fingers when it dries. You look for dead flowers to blow on. They break into downy tufts which fly away when the wind blows. You try to catch them. You run after them but they swerve aside just as you are about to touch them. You put buttercup corollas against your throat, you press them all along your neck, they are reflected in yellow spots up to the curve of the chin. You find daisies too. Their heavy heads pull them toward the ground and they get tangled together. You see them droop, their white petals are tightly sheathed by the dark green of their calyxes. You hear barking. It is Monsieur Pégas' dog. Inès says, He is tied up. It sounds as if he is choking himself by pulling on his chain. You stop picking flowers. Alain Trévise tiptoes behind the hedge to look into Monsieur Pégas' garden. He whistles through his fingers. This means that everything is all right. You feel like watching the river. You can just see it at the far end of the field. The water glistens, there is grass on each side. You sit down on the flat stones on the bank. Up close the water is the same color green as the grass. You can't see the bottom. Suddenly you hear Monsieur Pégas yelling, Get out of here. He yells something else which you don't understand and then, I'm warning you I'll untie the dog. You are in his field. You begin to run along the river. Denise Joubert is in the apple tree. She doesn't hear. You yell at the same time as Monsieur Pégas, Come on Denise, look out for the dog. Inès is in front. You yell. Then you can't yell any more because you are running. You have dropped flowers all over the field. They are on the grass, some of them still form the remains of bouquets, most of them are alone, scattered over all the distance you ran before your hands were completely empty. It is the big daisies standing on their heads that you can see best from a distance. You fall face down behind the hedge. You try to breathe. You see Denise Joubert jump out of the apple tree and start to run as fast as she can along the river. The dog is following her. Monsieur Pégas is following her. He is yelling, Filthy brat, thief, just wait until I catch you, I'll thrash you, just wait, thief. He has a stick. Denise Joubert runs beside the water trying to get out of Monsieur Pégas' meadow. The dog catches up with her. Monsieur Pégas is almost up to her too. You can hear his voice and the dog's barking together. Denise Joubert has no choice but to jump into the river. She swims against the current. The water is high. She has trouble swimming. Denise Joubert is not getting anywhere. You are afraid she will drown. Monsieur Pégas is still running, along the riverbank now, the dog is beside him, Filthy brat, wait until I get you, thief. He is waiting for her to come ashore. Denise Joubert has come closer to the bank. Monsieur Pégas is about to corner her. She is forced to stay in the water. You can see that the current is too strong for her. You yell, Denise, Denise. Inès runs off to find Denise Joubert's mother. Denise Joubert is going around in a circle because of the eddy. She is struggling against the current. She gains a little. She gains some more. Monsieur Pégas starts running again with his dog and his stick. It looks as if he is about to jump into the water after Denise Joubert. No, he retraces his steps and runs the other way. He turns around again, he runs up and down at the edge of the water, Filthy brat, thief, thief. He stamps his feet, he shakes his stick. Denise Joubert has almost passed the boundary of the field. She passes the boundary of the field. Monsieur Pégas comes too. He is going to wait for her on the other side of the hedge. You yell. You help Denise Joubert out of the water. She falls flat on her stomach. Her hair is sticking to her face and neck. Her clothes are sticking to her chest and arms. Water is running down her legs. You grab her by the shoulders. You begin to run almost carrying her. Monsieur Pégas is coming from behind. Monsieur Pégas is very close. The dog is by the hedge, barking. He stays in his own field but Monsieur Pégas doesn't. You meet Inès and Denise Joubert's enormous mother who can't run very fast. She goes up to Monsieur Pégas and begins to bawl him out because of her daughter, Disgusting old man, it looks as if she is going to jump on him and bash his head in. You tried to kill her, you pig, picking on children. Dirty rat, pig. Monsieur Pégas isn't yelling any more. He is much smaller than Denise Joubert's mother. Denise Joubert is catching her breath. You give her a pullover. She takes off her dress and puts it on. You don't run any more. You see Monsieur Pégas and his dog going away, followed by Denise Joubert's mother whom you can hear yelling. Catherine Legrand walks to school, holding Véronique Legrand by the hand. They walk along the path beside the national highway. They cross the highway at the supermarket, looking to the left and to the right to make sure the road is empty. When they are on the path Catherine Legrand lets go of Véronique Legrand's hand. The bicycles raise dust as they go by. The nettles, the thistles, the knot grass, those low leaves that look like rhubarb only wider, thicker and more wrinkled that grow beside the road are all full of dust. Véronique Legrand has blond hair that is almost white. She runs ahead on the path, you can see her knees touch her chin when she jumps. And her hair bounces above her forehead. You stop to make weewee because nobody is around. You squat down. You watch the urine make patterns in the dust, the little golden rills run around islands, then disappear under the thick leaves that look like rhubarb. Big flies buzz by. Véronique Legrand says, What is meat made of. It is made of the stuff in your nose, all the nasty things that are found in noses. That's not true. Yes it is. I'm going to ask Mama. You write in your notebook with a pen which you dip into purple ink. The point scrapes the paper, the two ends come apart, it is like writing on a blotter, afterward the nib is full of little hairs. You take them off with your fingers. You start writing again. There are more hairs. You rub the pen on your smock. You wipe it on the skin of your hand. You separate the two parts of the nib so you can get your finger between them and clean them. The pointed ends do not go back together again, so that now you write double. Catherine Legrand raises her finger. Mademoiselle, my pen is broken. Mademoiselle gets mad. That makes the third today, you must pay attention and hold your pen like this. Mademoiselle is standing behind Catherine Legrand. Mademoiselle leans over her shoulder to guide her hand. You are touching her with your head. She smells black and rough. You hold the pen between your thumb and index finger. Your index finger is bent at a right angle and presses against the round end the point is stuck into. Your thumb is a little less bent. The index finger is always sliding onto the inky point. In your notebook there are purple fingerprints, the lines made by inky fingers are spaced regularly in the shape of circles. You have to press the index finger against the end of the pen with all your might so it won't slide off. The thumb is also pressed to the end to keep the pen tight between the fingers, which then you can't use. Your whole arm even hurts. It is better to write with a pencil and to get rid of the pen by breaking it accidentally or losing it. Anyway Catherine Legrand is a pig. Mademoiselle tells her so waving her notebook, Do you know what this notebook is? A real pigpen. There are ink stains and fingerprints on the notebook. This is because when you dip the pen into the inkwell it either comes out full of ink or else without enough ink. In the first case the ink immediately drips onto the notebook just as you are getting ready to write. In the second case you press the nib of the pen onto the paper too hard and it makes holes. After this there is no point even trying to make the letters as you know how to do with a pencil. Françoise Pommier makes round, fine letters with her pen that stay right between the two lines without sticking out. Françoise Pommier writes slowly and carefully. At the top of her notebook she pushes a clean blotter along the line, holding it in place with the hand that is not writing. She raises her head when she has finished the page. She does not say, There, I'm finished. She waits for Mademoiselle to come over and look at her notebook. Mademoiselle is pleased with Françoise Pommier and gives her compliments. Pascale Delaroche makes a blot. She gives a little cry which she holds back by putting her hand over her mouth. Without raising her finger she asks for an eraser in a loud voice. Mademoiselle tells her to be quiet. I am coming, wait a moment please. She is looking at Reine Dieu's notebook. It has a lot of blots and holes like Catherine Legrand's. It also has doodles around which Reine Dieu has written the letters as she was asked to do. She has tried to erase something here and there. This makes a funny mess with hills and valleys which you want to touch. Between the hills it is dirty. Mademoiselle gets mad again and even throws Reine Dieu's notebook under the table. Reine Dieu is punished by having to kneel between the rows of desks. You can see her beige socks which have slipped down to her ankles, they form pleats below the red line that the elastic left in the place where it had stayed the longest. Reine Dieu looks all around, sits on her heels, straightens up, squints first up and then down, finally squints straight ahead, and crosses her eyes. Reine Dieu is on her knees in the aisle. She pulls at her belt, takes it off to play with it, drops it on the floor, hunts for it on all fours under the desks, asks Mademoiselle if she can go back to her seat, rummages in the pockets of her smock where she finds some pieces of string and a rubber band. Reine Dieu wrinkles her nose as she plays with the rubber band and the pieces of string. She puts the rubber band in her mouth and pulls it until she can hook it around the second button of her smock. It snaps in her face. Her hair is pulled way back on her head with a ribbon. It sticks out all over her head in frizzled locks. Véronique Legrand is sitting in the garden. Véronique Legrand is in her wicker chair. She is playing with a little stick which looks like an elbow because of the knot in the wood. She is telling herself a story, the little stick follows its ups and downs by sliding in her hand and performing all the movements she wants it to make. It whips between her fingers. Now it is still. Véronique Legrand stops talking and looks at it, pulling her tongue. She drops the stick, she gets down on all fours and looks for it, she finds it under the armchair. With her help it climbs up the wicker and takes its place on the seat. Véronique Legrand is on her knees in front of it and she begins to talk to it again. She leaves it on the chair. She crawls around in the dust on her hands and knees. She stops in front of another stick not much bigger than the first but without a knot. Véronique Legrand sits down beside it, picks it up, studies it, turning it over and over. Véronique Legrand does not say anything, Véronique Legrand goes over to the chair and puts the second stick beside the first. Véronique Legrand plays with the sticks. She finds them all in the garden and she lays them on the chair. When she has enough she takes them one at a time and plants them in the ground. She moves them around according to a system which she invents as she goes along, either in a straight line, or two by two, or all together without any order. Catherine Legrand is turning round and round in the garden. Alain Trévise's father is in front of the wood-pile. He is hitting an iron bar with a hammer. He is squatting. The bar is in front of him on the beaten ground. He strikes regularly. The clang of metal against metal can be heard all over the garden. Catherine Legrand goes to the garden fence. There is nobody on the road. Catherine Legrand tries to stick her head through the bars. On the other side of the road, way behind the big empty fields without flowers and full of sharp and colorless grass, you can see some high flat houses. The fields are broken up by long fences of wooden pickets held together by iron wire. The pickets are loosely joined, there are spaces as wide as two or three pickets between them. The loose iron wire does not hold them all. Some which have come undone hang crookedly and droop to the ground. Others have collapsed completely or disappeared, blown away by the wind or taken by people, you see only a wider space where they would normally be. Alain Trévise's father has stopped hitting the iron bar. You hear the bar fall to the ground, then the hammer which hits it as it falls. You hear the sound of scrap iron being moved. Catherine Legrand goes up the path, jumping with both feet. She bends down to watch a slug among the sunflowers. You turn it over with a stone, squeeze it, it spurts, moves slowly in all directions, you press on it, it spreads and re-enfolds itself. Véronique Legrand's sticks are now in a circle. Véronique Legrand sucks some little pebbles to make them clean and after that she piles them inside the circle she has made with the sticks, they are all white, one beside or on top of the other. You go on a pilgrimage to Mandorle with Mademoiselle. You walk in line two by two. Catherine Legrand is next to Reine Dieu. In front of her is Hélène Corte next to Françoise Pommier. Behind her is Pascale Delaroche with Jacqueline Marchand. You pass the church where you go to mass on Sunday. You come to the national highway. You do not pass the supermarket. You pass the hardware store where there are red and green balloons tied together. You are in front of Sophie Jamain's house. Mademoiselle walks up the rows. She stops beside Sophie Jamain, bends over and says something to her that you can't hear. She gives the signal to halt. Mademoiselle crosses the road, she goes into Sophie Jamain's house. You sit on the sidewalk. Reine Dieu hops ahead. Sophie Jamain runs across the street, she stands in front of the door of her house and looks at the others. After a moment she goes back to the sidewalk and jumps on the edge touching it first with her left foot then with her right foot, so that her right foot is on the sidewalk when her left foot is on the road and vice versa, this is how she waits for Mademoiselle to come back out of her house. Pascale Delaroche is on the wall of the house across from Sophie Jamain's. She is cutting a lilac branch, her hand is between the bars of the fence. Mademoiselle comes out and you line up again. Once again you walk on the national highway. You pass houses that you don't know on the right and on the left. There are gardens with fences, sometimes stone steps, in front of them. You don't see the houses that you are passing. You are talking. You are tired. You see that there aren't any houses on either side of the road. Mademoiselle gives the sign that you may halt. You go into a field. Reine Dieu tickles the inside of her nose with a big piece of grass which she has torn up by the roots. She tickles the inside of Catherine Legrand's nose too. Catherine Legrand struggles, tries to grab hold of it, the grass goes into her ears and neck. You are under a big apple tree. Mademoiselle says she is going to tell a story. You are sitting around her. It is the story of a holy little boy who was stoned to death when he tried to take the host of Our Lord to a sick person. The host was found between his shirt and skin where it had been hidden. You begin walking on the road again. Catherine Legrand's shoes are full of dirt and she has dirt under her fingernails from the holes she dug under the apple tree. Mademoiselle wants you to sing because when you sing you aren't tired. You sing, To walk a mile wears out wears out to walk a mile wears out your shoes, left, left. When you say left you have to be on your left foot. You have to change feet by making a little jump so as to be on the correct foot. The best way of marching which must be our way. Reine Dieu begins to drag behind. Catherine Legrand next to her sees that Pascale Delaroche and Jacqueline Marchand are passing them, singing as they go. You start to look for nuts and bolts by the edge of the road. Reine Dieu says sometimes they fall off of trucks. With your feet you shove aside the dry leaves the dust the old scraps of newspaper which are in the gutter. You walk on the tar road, stamping your feet one after the other. Reine Dieu shakes her head from right to left. She holds out her arms and catches Catherine Legrand who is walking around her sideways like a crab. Reine Dieu grabs the collar of Catherine Legrand's jacket and Catherine Legrand grabs the buttons of Reine Dieu's blouse. You shake with all your might, you try to knock each other down. You laugh. You twist around all doubled up. Catherine Legrand's jacket which Reine Dieu is pulling off is stuck on her head. She is underneath trying to wriggle free she is holding onto a button of Reine Dieu's blouse. Mademoiselle notices that Catherine Legrand and Reine Dieu are no longer in line. You hear a whistle blast. You see that the others are far away that you can't hear them that they look smaller than when you are next to them. Mademoiselle is waving her arms, you have to run in order to catch up with them. When you are almost up to them you hear Mademoiselle yelling so you stop running and drag your feet. Reine Dieu is standing in front of Mademoiselle with her head bowed. She puts her feet which are together farther and farther apart, she puts the right one forward, she begins to paw the road slowly with her shoe from front to back. When Mademoiselle has finished you go to the head of the line where she tells you to go. You drag your feet the others are singing, Left left, a toad he lived in a pumpkin shell. There is a big field with some weeds with pink blossoms and some sky-blue flowers that are just as tall as the grass. These are either flax flowers or wolfsbane. Each corolla is closely joined to the next and at the same time separate from it, the outlines are very sharp, which gives the whole flower, the whole field a geometric look.

You go into the field of flowers. You have arrived. You roll in the grass. It is dry in places but damp at the bottom. There is a sour smell, there are other more sweetish smells, the result is a mixture that you inhale with pleasure. You pick flowers, taking the whole stalks. Reine Dieu breaks off the blossoms and puts them in her mouth. She tears up the flowers as she runs without stopping and spitting the first ones out and replacing them with others. Reine Dieu stuffs her mouth with flowers, she is choking on them, you can see blue shreds of crushed petal on her lips and wedged between her teeth. You scare away butterflies that you don't see, they are the same color as the flax flowers or wolfsbane. The chapel is on the other side of the national highway on a little hill of bare ground. The sun is low in the field. It makes the stones of the chapel pink. Mademoiselle says, That's all now we're going to the chapel. Reine Dieu crawls to the highway. Mademoiselle turns her back on her. Catherine Legrand catches up with her. Reine Dieu and Catherine Legrand hide behind the chapel. You are reading whole sentences aloud out of the book. Mademoiselle is sitting in the wicker chair behind the big desk which comes all the way to the floor so you can't see her legs. She is reading from the same book as yours. Denise Baume is repeating a sentence. Hélène Corte has already read this sentence but she could not finish it. The trea-sure that the poor fa-mi-ly found in the well was an un-ex- un-ex-, Denise Baume stumbles too. Mademoiselle taps with her ruler making little dry sounds on the desk, Begin again. Denise Baume begins the sentence again. The trea-sure that the poor fa-mi-ly found in the well was an un-ex-, Denise Baume stops at the same place in the sentence. Mademoiselle says un-ex- what? Françoise Pommier raises her finger. Mademoiselle looks to see if any other fingers are raised in the classroom. She repeats, un-ex- what, what does it mean, Reine Dieu, un-ex- what? Reine Dieu looks at Mademoiselle, Reine Dieu looks around. Françoise Pommier raises her finger. You see Reine Dieu stir on the bench, you see her start to struggle to her feet. Reine Dieu repeats, un-ex- what? Mademoiselle shrugs her shoulders. Mademoiselle nods to Françoise Pommier that she may speak. Françoise Pommier recites the end of the sentence by heart without looking at the book, was an un-ex-pec-ted stroke of luck. Mademoiselle tells Denise Baume to continue. It was just like this a while ago they stopped for a long time over the word fa-mi-ly. They said *fa* then *mi* then *ly*. Mademoiselle's lips disappear into her mouth, pulling the skin on her cheeks tight, she leans on her forearms, her head is rigid when she looks at the class to the left or to the right, you can see her bun very round on the top of her head, in front of it her hair is pulled back so tightly it looks as if the hairs are about to snap. Catherine Legrand is with Reine Dieu in the play-ground. You are collecting little yellow pebbles your pockets are full of them. Who wants yellow pebbles who wants yellow pebbles? You yell, stamping your feet one after the other so that you raise your legs high. You take the pebbles and fling them against the wooden doors of the toilet. The doors are green with grooves. At first you throw them from a distance and one at a time. You come closer and eventually you have to throw them point blank and in handfuls. You hear them land inside where they bounce from one wall to another. They go in through the heart-shaped opening. Mademoiselle comes and yells, Will you come out of there. You run away. Reine Dieu pulls the belt of Catherine Legrand who is running ahead of her. You go into the little children's play-ground. Véronique Legrand is sitting on the ground. She has taken the shoelaces out of both shoes, she has also taken off her shoes, she is sitting in the dust in her stocking feet. Véronique Legrand is trying to thread a lace into one of the shoes, she is concentrating so hard that she is sticking out her tongue, Véronique Legrand gives up, she puts the shoe aside, she starts making knots in the shoelace, her tongue hangs out of her mouth. Reine Dieu puts her hands over her face, Guess who. Véronique Legrand doesn't know who it is she tries to push away the hands that cover her eyes, her little fingers cling to and tangle with Reine Dieu's, which are much bigger than hers. Véronique Legrand does not say a word, you can see that Véronique Legrand is laughing silently. Catherine Legrand and Reine Dieu take her by the hand. They swing her with their hands. They say Swing, Véronique Legrand. They let her go because the bell rings. Catherine and Véronique Legrand go to school hand in hand. Véronique Legrand doesn't like cars. You look ahead and behind every few minutes to see if one is coming. When one comes along Véronique Legrand goes to the side of the road even if it is still far away and flattens herself against the wooden picket fence. Véronique Legrand sees cars go by in an endless single file. It so happens that these cars are full of evil intentions, as a matter of fact it is very dangerous to walk on the sidewalk where one is always in danger of meeting a car. They pretend they really don't see anything, they pretend to be blind and to pass peacefully by you on the road and all of a sudden when you think they have gone by they turn and run you over in your tracks. It is dark it is all closed in you hear the sound they make only when they are very near or when they have gone by, it always makes a breeze. Véronique Legrand is in the garden. When she looks behind her, she sees a big truck coming toward her without making any noise. She walks backward waving her hands in front of her so the driver will see she is there. She sees that there isn't any driver. There are only the two big eyes on the front of the hood looking at her. The truck comes toward her very slowly. Véronique Legrand walks away as fast as she can. Backwards it isn't easy. She realizes that she can't back up any farther because she is against the wall. The truck comes closer and closer it is very close. If Véronique Legrand holds out her arms she

can touch it, but Véronique Legrand doesn't want to
hold out her arms, she hides them behind her back
instead, it is about to touch her it is about to run
her over Véronique Legrand scrunches down against
the wall and just as the truck is about to touch her
does touch her begins to run her over she starts to
scream with all her might. You are sitting in a meadow.
There is a tablecloth on the grass, and plates. Véronique Legrand has an orange-and-blue checked napkin around her neck. She is drinking water out of a
big glass which she is holding with both hands. You
can see her tongue inside she is pressing it against the
side, around the place where the tongue is squashed
against the glass there is a greenish fringe caused
by suction. Mother wipes Véronique Legrand's mouth
with the end of the napkin which is knotted around
her neck. Father cuts off a hazel branch and makes
designs on the bark with his penknife. The wood
underneath is all white and damp when you touch it.
Finally the stick is completely stripped of its bark,
the white yellows after a moment so you wrap handkerchiefs around it to keep it white. Some white and
rust-colored cows come near as they graze. Beside
the nearest one there is another one a little farther
back followed by another one who is eating the grass
almost between the legs of the one in front of her.
Every once in a while one of them raises her head,
saliva runs down her muzzle to the dewlaps and some
half-chewed grass, the remains of clover and lucerne
with those pink flowers that look like pompons. To

43

start feeding again the cow nuzzles a long bunch of grass, blowing or sniffling at the same time with a soft, moist sound. The cow with the shortest horns is beside the tablecloth. She relieves herself of a round, flat mound of dung that steams. Her tail is arched in the air. Beneath it something opens and another piece of dung falls beside the first, only smaller. When the cow has finished the tail falls back she thrusts her head forward and pulls on it turning it from side to side and gives a long moo which stretches her neck more and more until it is over. Then the head is like it was before. You pull up the grass in handfuls. You feed the cow with your hand making sure that your fingers are straight. The tongue caresses your palms, it is rough and wet with saliva. When you come home from school in the afternoon the sun is sinking behind the field with the short grass and no flowers, it is sinking behind the fences and the wooden pickets. You can't see anything but the front of the big buildings, the windows side by side shine red, this is the only place you can see that there is some sunlight left, it makes one big mass of red and fire, you have to squint. In these houses live tiny men and women whose faces you can't see because they are covered with blood, they are born that way. They are inside the houses which look like card houses. You can also see them crawling between the houses, this is when they go in and come out of their houses. You must force yourself to look the other way, away from the setting sun, where the grass is almost black, where you do not see water flowing through the fields. You aren't allowed to watch them, in fact if you go any farther they come in the night, you dream that the men with no skin on their bloody faces come to your bed and without looking at you put their hands on your throat to strangle and kill you. In Catherine Legrand's class there is a new pupil whose name is Suzanne Mériel. She is very tall. Her blond hair is like after a permanent, it is parted in the middle of her head and hangs from barrettes on both sides, it would look like spaniel's ears except it's curly. Her cheeks are purplish. You call her mop girl. Even though Suzanne Mériel is a big girl she can't read or write. Mademoiselle laughs at her. Then Suzanne Mériel says something but what she says isn't really words, it sounds like low, hoarse whimpering. She has to sit on a bench all by herself. You can see scabs on her head. Josiane Fourmont says they are lice. You look for her lice. You hit her with your rulers. You hit her on the back and head. She hunches her back and pulls her head into her shoulders. She makes no other movement. You hit her harder. You hear the low, hoarse voice that comes out of her steadily. You beat her. The blows resound on her head, on her back. All the rulers in the class land on her back, on her whole body. You beat in rhythm, everyone at once, you yell. Now she is covering her head with her arms, her elbows stick out in front of her face and are hit by the rulers. The voice continues to come out of her in time to the blows, low and steady. You laugh. You wait for her after school. You want to throw stones at her. Inès takes her by the hand and puts her arm around her shoulders. Suzanne Mériel begins to cry the tears run down her purplish, mottled cheeks. You hear the sobs, you hear the husky voice. You walk after them at a distance. You hear Inès talking with Suzanne Mériel now, you hear her start to yell when you try to come near. At a distance you follow Suzanne Mériel who walks holding onto Inès. You see them leave this way every afternoon and arrive this way every morning. Inès accompanies Suzanne Mériel to the door of the classroom and leaves her only when Mademoiselle gives the sign that the class has begun. And she waits at the door for her at noon and in the afternoon, talking only to her and accompanying her to the door of her house. In the garden Véronique Legrand is crushing bricks to build a house. Catherine Legrand is at the fence with her head wedged between the bars. On the road she sees an uncovered moving van go by. The furniture is piled up every which way behind the cab. There are all kinds of furniture: stoves tables chairs sofas mirrors cupboards. Catherine Legrand sees that at the bottom the whole structure is supported by a little boy who is balancing a huge wardrobe on his head, several chairs are also on his outstretched arms, as well as a center table. He is naked, and looks very sick. On closer inspection Catherine Legrand sees that there is another little boy who is also in the furniture but toward the middle of the structure. His neck is twisted because his head is turned, he must have turned it at the last minute just as someone was putting something on his head and it was already too late to put it back in place. The little boys are both as still as statues, for the slightest movement would endanger the balance of the whole. Both of them are naked. The truck drives very slowly but you can't see the little boys from behind. Catherine Legrand runs back up the path. Véronique Legrand doesn't listen to what Catherine Legrand tells her. She has now reduced two bricks to powder. Véronique Legrand spits on the powder, she mixes the powder with saliva. It makes a thick pink mortar which she stirs with a stone she has in her hand. After a minute she runs out of saliva and asks Catherine Legrand to spit on it too. Very carefully Véronique Legrand covers several stones with pink paste. Catherine Legrand is on the wall looking toward town. Catherine Legrand sees Inès on the widest of the roads. Inès is surrounded with children jumping up and down in the coal dust. She has just gone to buy bread. A big black market bag is hanging from her arm which she holds folded against her side. She has taken out one of the loaves of bread and is breaking it by pulling at the part where there isn't any crust. This makes a big hole through which you can see the soft part of the bread. When Catherine Legrand turns around she sees that Véronique Legrand is still busy grinding brick. In the laundry the tubs are gray and patinaed and slippery to the touch. One of them contains a transparent green liquid. You can reach the tub by overturning a basin and dragging it up, the edge of the basin scraping against the stone of the floor makes a metallic sound. If you stand on the overturned basin which sags in the middle and lean way over you can get some of the liquid in the hollow of your hand, it looks like absinthe but it has a piney taste that sets your teeth on edge. Reine Dieu is absent. Mademoiselle makes a cross in the column beside her name. You are having dictation. Catherine Legrand doesn't have time to write all the words that Mademoiselle says. You leave spaces as big as you think the words are. You will try to fill them when Mademoiselle rereads the dictation. The pen jumps from one unfinished word to the next, leaving another blank space. The pen continues to be disobedient in the hand that holds it. The point of the pen is always misbehaving, bending and dividing into two very distinct parts. You dip the pen into the inkwell, you shake it to get rid of the excess ink, you carry it to the notebook. The point catches the paper, makes letters that tear the paper and come out broken ragged and messy. You write sea, shoe, school, you skip a word that you didn't have time to write and didn't remember then you write mimosa, meter, mountain, mass, you skip another word ending in on, maybe it was mason. You wait for Mademoiselle to reread the dictation. By paying close attention you manage to fill one or two spaces but no more and you do this only by ignoring the rest of what she reads so you aren't even sure that the words you wrote next are the right ones. After each word Mademoiselle says comma, wall comma, house comma, you hurry to write the missing words while she is saying comma but there isn't enough time to fill in all the missing words. Mademoiselle says, Reread your dictation. Mademoiselle says, Eyes on your notebooks and not out the window, eyes on your notebooks and not on the blackboard, whenever you look up. Mademoiselle chooses someone to collect the notebooks. Everyone raises her finger and calls, Me, mademoiselle, me. Mademoiselle says, Josiane Fourmont, collect the notebooks. The others grumble. You hear remarks here and there. Mademoiselle makes several sharp taps with her ruler to restore silence. Josiane Fourmont goes through the rows with a pile of notebooks. Pascale Delaroche says something to her in a low voice as she hands her hers. You hear whispers, the sound of pens being laid on desks or dropped, desks scraping, clothes rubbing against wood. You are restless the room is not completely silent. You half rise, you sit down again. This is the pause that precedes the moment when Mademoiselle will say, And now we are going to. You are in the playground. Some big girls are forcing some smaller ones to play with them. The little ones will be the patients, the big ones are the doctors. You wait your turn in line. The elderberry trees in the corner of the wall give off a sickening sour smell. You pick the berries which make your teeth black. Jacqueline Marchand says this is what ink is made from. You spit out the pulp and skin at the same time. You don't like the taste of elderberries it's too sugary, too sweetish and also it reminds you of ether. You are afraid of being poisoned. Mademoiselle says ink is poisonous. Monique Despiaud comes for the pupils one at a time for the examination. You follow her. You are with the other big girls. You hear a voice say, Take off your clothes. You obey. Monique Despiaud takes off your panties which you kept on. Monique Despiaud says, Kneel against the wall. You are afraid. You kneel. You look at the wall, it's thin and shiny about two meters high it looks like a pediment and forms an angle with another wall which is just the same but not as long, both walls are stuck in the middle of the school vegetable patch, as if to make a playhouse for Monique Despiaud Luce Fourmont Nicole Blatier. You feel a hand on your naked and exposed buttocks. A sharp pain a little above the anus is caused by a stick or some pointed object which may be of metal. You don't scream. Monique Despiaud takes Catherine Legrand's hand and helps her put her clothes back on. Josiane Fourmont's sister Luce Fourmont says, The operation is over, next. You go back to the elderberry tree to the others who are awaiting their turns behind the wall. Nicole Blatier is there to keep them from seeing what is going on on the other side of the wall. Denise Baume breaks a branch with her teeth, tears off the bark and shows the marrow which she pulls out without breaking it. Denise Baume says it's good to eat. You eat some elderberry marrow, it gets stuck in your teeth. Mademoiselle crosses the playground and comes toward the angle formed by the two walls which Monique Despiaud Luce Fourmont Nicole Blatier are inside of. Nicole Blatier sees her coming and gives a little whistle to warn the others. Everyone leaves the hideout Monique Despiaud Luce Fourmont Nicole Blatier walk slowly toward the little girls under the elderberry tree, Françoise Pommier Jacqueline Marchand Catherine Legrand Denise Baume, whom they start pretending to examine. Now they use an open hoop to encircle one or the other of the little girls, tightening the circle of metal around her waist once they have managed to get one of them inside it. Seeing that the game is harmless, Mademoiselle walks away. You are having your afternoon nap. It is warm in bed. You can't sleep. In her bed Véronique Legrand is playing with her fingers. While she does it she hums a kind of song on one note. It sounds like ai-ai-ai-ai-ai, monotonous and sustained. She holds both hands in front of her eyes. She separates the fingers one at a time. She holds two of them pressed together. She keeps them like that for a while. She lets them go. Separates them quickly. She chooses one, the index, which she grabs with the other hand. She looks at it. It walks slowly on the fold of the sheet. It falls into a valley, stands up again, limps a little, starts off again at a run. It leaves the ground and begins to fly, slowly at first, then faster and faster, until finally it crashes on the ground where it lies, broken. Véronique Legrand abandons it and turns her attention to two other

fingers one of which is decidedly bigger than the
other. There are the middle finger and the little
finger. They move together and stand for Véronique
Legrand and Catherine Legrand, one walks a little
behind the other because it is smaller. They go to
school walking on the sidewalk like good girls. They
pull over to the side when a car goes by. The little
one puts her foot in a puddle, the big one scolds her.
The little one keeps on putting her feet in the puddle
anyway. The other one pulls her by the hand. But
suddenly the big one changes her mind and begins to
stamp in the puddle too, pushing the little one away
so as to have all the room. The little one puts up a
good fight. They are now both splashing around in
the same puddle. They are playing with little pebbles
in the playground. The idea is to take little white
pebbles which you have sucked first to make them
clean and put them in all the openings you have. You
begin with the mouth, then comes the nose. They do
not stay very long in the nose. You can put several
of them in your ears at the same time. The little one
is worried, one of the pebbles is stuck in her ear but
the big one gets it out and they start over. Catherine
Legrand is bored in bed it is hot and she can't sleep.
Catherine Legrand does not play with her fingers. In
a little while she will go to the daisy field with Inès
and Denise Joubert. You are made at Alain Trévise.
Denise Joubert is holding onto Marie-José Venant
who lives very near her house. Marie-José Venant
has long pigtails that come down to her stomach. You

are making daisy chains. Inès shows how to put them together putting all the heads the same way. You play Queen. Marie-José Venant is the holy queen. She kneels down. You put a crown of daisies on her head. You take her by the hand to escort her to her throne on the molehill. Marie-José Venant sits very stiff the way a queen should and also to keep her crown on. You fix her train around her. You stick daisies into the top of her dress. She has a stick which she holds straight in front of her. You take turns bowing to her. You bend over very low and walk away backward. You throw daisies, cornflowers, buttercups, dandelions in her face as you saw done for the monstrance at Corpus Christi. You throw them faster and faster, she gets excited, she laughs, she rolls on the ground, you throw flowers at Denise Joubert, at Inès, your hair is full of them, you roll on the ground. You are on the porch. It is raining outside. You can't see the rain dripping off the branches of the cypress trees. But all the way down the windowpanes raindrops run one after the other. They stick to the glass and stay there. Sometimes one raindrop swallows another which it met by chance, fatter now it begins to slide faster and faster across the pane. On the porch Catherine Legrand and Véronique Legrand are sorting out their toys. Mother says, There is no more room you must throw away all the toys that are broken. You are sorting. To the right you put everything you agree to give up, to the left you pile the toys you want to keep. In the bad pile the discard pile there is almost nothing so far, some breadcrusts, a few torn scraps of paper, some unusable boxes. The good pile gets everything. You can't throw away a toy just because it's broken. Toys you abandon cry at night while you are asleep it says so in your reader. For this reason the good pile contains dogs with missing legs, dolls' heads, headless tin soldiers, nuts, pictures, boxes, cars with and without wheels and other toys that are almost new. Marbles have rolled into every corner. Véronique Legrand goes back and forth between the two piles. Out of the bad pile she fishes a stick or a box which she decides is still usable and brings it over to the good pile. Sometimes on the windowpane a raindrop that is fatter than the rest runs straight down but more often slantways they glisten they are like trains speeding by in the night. Mother says there are still way too many things, start over. The porch is littered with toys from one end to the other. To move around you have to step over the single toys and the piles being careful not to step on a smaller toy or a pencil or a marble. Véronique Legrand hides several objects behind the boiler of the central heating system to save them from the purge. You see an agate roll slowly from between two open boxes and head for the corner of the wall by the door. The door is level with the garden. There is a gravel path around the lawn and the two plum trees. The two trees make the light on the porch green. When it rains the green is darker. There are all kinds of pipes in the porch going back and forth between the bathroom on the one side the kitchen on the other. Véronique feels way down in the good pile to find the wooden puppet. A little orange spider is climbing up her neck. Finally when she can't find it she sits down on the floor and cries. Inès and Denise Joubert are waving their arms in the field. When you come closer they say that Marie-José Venant is dead. You go with them to the front of Marie-José Venant's house. In the kitchen the mother is preparing string beans. On the oilcloth there is a newspaper on which Marie-José Venant's mother puts the strings which she pulls from one end of the beans to the other with the point of her knife. She sits at the table crying as she works. Her tears run down her cheeks onto her apron onto the edge of the paper. Marie-José Venant is lying on the bed in the next room. A veil of white net is stretched over her. A crown of white roses has been placed on her head. In her hands which are clasped over the two black braids which have been laid on her chest she is holding a rosary of mother-of-pearl beads. Her eyes are closed. Her cheeks are as white as ever. You take a palm branch from a glass containing holy water beside the bed, you dip it into the holy water and lift it over the bed making the sign of the cross. A few drops of holy water make the net sag. The mother has come in silently on tiptoe. She chases the flies away from the net with a dishcloth then she hides her face in it because she has begun to sob. When she takes it away you see that her cheeks are all red and flushed. She can hardly speak. She says that you can stay there for another moment, that it makes her happy. Her sobs get louder and louder. She leaves the room. You are standing up. You are not talking. You look at Marie-José Venant under the net. When you go through the kitchen again on your way out the mother is still preparing the string beans. In front of her on the newspaper there is a little almost transparent pile of strings, ends, and those little hoods that join the hulls of the beans to the beanstalk. Marie-José Venant's mother takes a handkerchief out of the pocket of her apron and dabs at her eyes. Inès says, Don't get up Madame. You leave her sitting down. As you go down the steps you can hear her crying loudly.

Reine Dieu is at the blackboard. She is making a mess of her multiplication. The board is behind Mademoiselle's platform, so that Mademoiselle turns halfway around in her chair and twists her neck to watch her. From the side you can see her bun and half of her glasses, one of the steel rims with glass in it. The frame is hooked behind her ear. You can see it clearly because her hair is pulled back by the bun. Reine Dieu erases the result of her multiplication with her fingers. It makes a white blur in which you can still read one or two figures, there are damp fingerprints in the middle. Reine Dieu is standing on one foot. This doesn't help her. She shifts to the other. Mademoiselle turns to the rest of the class. She explains the principle of multiplication one more time. Reine Dieu leans her back against the blackboard. She is very close to Mademoiselle. She comes still closer. Reine Dieu leans forward to look at Mademoiselle's bun. There are a lot of white hairs in it. Some of them have come loose from the bun. Reine Dieu touches them with the tips of her fingers. She waves her hand lightly up and down around Mademoiselle's head. At a movement from Mademoiselle Reine Dieu scratches her head with her index finger and puts her hands into the pocket of her blouse. Mademoiselle doesn't notice anything. She says, Take your scratch pads and do the multiplication on the blackboard. While you are copying it into your notebooks, Mademoiselle looks at the multiplication behind her. Reine Dieu takes a step backward the moment Mademoiselle turns her head. When she sees that Mademoiselle has her eyes on the class once again, Reine Dieu goes up behind her very quickly and snap! pulls out the white hair that is sticking out. This time Mademoiselle has felt something. Mademoiselle jumps up. She is all red. She can hardly talk. She says, Why did you do that? Reine Dieu is sorry to have put Mademoiselle into such a state. She doesn't answer. She hangs her head, her chin touches her chest. She sways from one foot to the other. Mademoiselle yells louder and louder. At last Reine Dieu says, But Mademoiselle, it was a white hair. Jacqueline Marchand leans over toward Pascale Delaroche and asks her if she saw Reine Dieu pull the teacher's hair, she says Oh and puts her hand over her mouth. You are playing tag. Reine Dieu is throwing handfuls of pebbles at Josiane Fourmont. Just as she is about to catch her Josiane Fourmont jumps over the wall, on the road she yells, You can't catch me, you can't catch me, she hops along the road with both feet. Reine Dieu runs after everyone at once. Denise Baume has just slipped away from her without getting tagged. Jacqueline Marchand slaps her on the back, but when Reine Dieu turns around she is far away. Françoise Pommier is a good way off and manages to stay that way. Josiane Fourmont is back in the playground. Reine Dieu runs after her as soon as she sees her. She is about to catch her, she has almost touched her back by the door to the toilet. Josiane Fourmont dashes inside and shuts the door. Reine Dieu beats on the wood of the door with her fists. Josiane Fourmont has thrown the bolt. She yells that she can't open the door. Reine Dieu throws her right shoulder against it with all her might. Josiane Fourmont gets excited. You can hear her wailing. You can hear her pulling at the latch. Françoise Pommier goes to tell Mademoiselle that Josiane Fourmont is locked in the toilet and can't get out. Josiane Fourmont can only move the latch a millimeter at a time. You can't hear her any more. Reine Dieu continues to hurl her shoulder against the door with all her might. Finally the catch twists, it gives way, the door opens all of a sudden and Reine Dieu, thrown forward by the impetus of her attack, bumps violently into Josiane Fourmont. Josiane Fourmont teeters on top of the toilet bowl and one of her legs plunges in up to the calf. She pulls out a foot smeared with a brown paste which slips between her shoelaces and soaks her white wool sock. It has a foul smell. It is shit mixed with water and urine. Josiane Fourmont comes out of the toilet on one foot. She holds the dirty foot in front of her. She looks at it, making a face and beginning to cry. When Mademoiselle comes over she sees that Josiane Fourmont has hidden her head in the crook of her arm against the wooden door and that she is holding as high as she can a foot, a shoe, a leg that is covered with shit halfway up the calf. You are taking a hike in the forest. You cross the square in front of the temple. You are lined up two by two. Denise Baume is next to Josiane Fourmont. In front of them are Catherine Legrand and Reine Dieu. In the middle of the square you see a bandstand. The main street is crowded with people on bicycles and in cars. You walk to the right on the edge of the sidewalk. You watch the people go around the concrete platform which marks off a big space on the square where cars aren't allowed to go. You turn left along the river. You walk two by two well to the right so as not to block traffic. You have crossed the most crowded part. There are no more stores. You still pass a house from time to time. The river is on the right. The houses are on the left on the other side of the road. The banks of the river come right to the poplar trees. They form dirt benches which slope gently down to the surface of the water. The grassy parts alternate with wide paths of hard clay which the heat bakes into an intricate network, swollen diamonds lying side by side. Sometimes the ruts are so deep you can almost see the fire that is inside the earth. On the other side of the river there is the row of poplars against the highway and behind higher up on the hills those trees of a spinachy green whose shapes you can't make out. On the highest of the hills you see the farmhouse in the boxwood grove. It is a tiny little white house seen from below. It reminds you of the song, Way up on the mountain there was an old chalet. You cross the river by a bridge and you keep going in the same direction toward the farmhouse. You go up a narrow unpaved road with hairpin turns. When you drag your feet along the ground you raise a white dust. When you see the farmhouse you can't see the river, and vice versa. The river gets farther and farther away and the house is much bigger now that you are nearer to it. There are no boxwood trees around the farmhouse. A walk made of earth and pebbles crushed so fine they look like sand forms the yard. When you have walked across this you enter the forest behind the farmhouse. You walk along a rutted road. You aren't in line any more. You run. You scatter. Reine Dieu crawls into the underbrush although you aren't allowed to leave the road. She collects beechnuts in her beret. You sit down on the ground in the middle of the road to eat them. They are little berries in the shape of tetrahedrons which have prickly corners and rounded swelling sides. It takes a long time to shell them and the fruit is very small. You walk along the road. There are beech trees, elm trees, ash, flowering ash, aspen. From time to time you come upon a clump of birch trees that looks like a little forest inside a bigger one. Leaves from an earlier year form a thick layer of humus in the underbrush which overflows and makes a thinner layer on the sides of the road and in the depressions made by the ruts or sometimes covers the whole width of the road. It sticks to the soles of your shoes you have to clean them off with a stick. You find sticks here and there in the underbrush or even in the middle of the road. They all look like dead wood. A few are big enough to make walking sticks. You lean on them with all your might to test their strength. Some break. These are the soft ones. The wood is rotten. You begin to make switches by cutting off hazel branches with your pocket knives. You don't even need a knife if you do it right the branch breaks off clean, this is the way to do it because it's too bendy and sharp to hold in your bare hand. You get them as long as possible. You take off the bark. You get the bendy ones. You hit tree trunks with them as you go by. When you find one that is too big to be easily handled, you throw it as far as you can. You hold it out to take aim then you let it fly. You make a plan. Mademoiselle is up ahead on the road. She is talking to Jacqueline Marchand and Françoise Pommier who have been walking beside her ever since you entered the forest. Josiane Fourmont Denise Baume Catherine Legrand Reine Dieu advance each carrying a stick. They run slowly bending their knees. Reine Dieu gives a whoop and all the sticks are thrown. Reine Dieu's flies over Mademoiselle's head and sticks in the ground in front of her. Mademoiselle gives a start and turns around yelling at the four little girls. You grab your beret and start to run. You would like to recover the sticks whose ends you went to the trouble of whittling. So you hide in the underbrush behind the bushes alongside Mademoiselle, Françoise Pommier and Jacqueline Marchand. After you leave the shelter of the bushes you crawl forward on your stomach, you reach the road without being seen, you get up yelling, you make a dash for the sticks. Mademoiselle begins to yell again but you have all the sticks. You find a bomb hole full of water. It looks like a little sea. The sides are covered with lichens, little red chickweed flowers and sedge are growing right in the middle of the water. When you stir the water with a stick it gets all muddy the dirt comes up from the bottom. You stir very fast. Several of you go at it. At last you get a thick substance which is almost mud. The water bugs that dart constantly over the surface and go backward when the stick comes toward them have disappeared. They have flown away, they have either climbed up the nearest tree trunks or the leaves of the bushes or they have gotten mixed into the peaty paste. In the woods are dead branches, the lower branches of prickly bushes—holly, eglantine, blackberry, brambles—dry leaves which the wind tosses and carries here and there in little mounds, yellow crocuses or pinkish-white hellebores or mauve cyclamens. You can't make a bouquet out of these kinds of flowers. The stems are too short and don't go together. Besides they are too heavy and half of them are hollow and slippery. You pick them anyway, the stems get squashed in your hand, you drop them one by one as your fingers loosen, in the end you drop them in smaller and smaller bunches on the road or throw them into the underbrush. By the time you get home in the evening the light is already gone under the trees. The palms of your hands are raw, your fingers are covered with scratches. You can't take another step. Mademoiselle is very busy. She walks back and forth beside the rows. She says you must sing to help you march. You sing, Don't cry Jeannette, he'll marry you, he'll marry you. It is dusk, the trees are half frozen and all black. When you leave the forest you see Venus in a sky that is still blue, though it is paler where the sun has set. You go back down the winding road to the river. You leave the farmhouse with the box grove behind. In the distance you hear sheep bells from a flock moving somewhere on the side of the hill. You hear shouts. The floor of the valley is already darkened. The river is a dull black path. You sing less and less loudly. Reine Dieu doesn't sing at all. Beside her Catherine

Legrand sings halfheartedly. Mademoiselle says, Come on, move, hurry, walk faster. You aren't allowed to go straight home. For instance Anne-Marie Losserand goes right by her own house. She says there is light in the kitchen and dining room. She wants to stop. Mademoiselle says you don't have time. You have to go back to school and get the books and notebooks you need to do tomorrow's lessons. Then you can go home. Mademoiselle is sick. There is a substitute whose name is Madame La Porte. She doesn't have glasses. She doesn't have a bun. She doesn't wear black. She has big round eyes. She has short curls all over her head. She wears lipstick. She smiles all the time. She says she doesn't know anyone but that she has the list of names. I shall call the roll. You will each rise as your name is called so I can get to know you. You get up and stand beside the bench for a moment. Madame La Porte studies each little girl and smiles at her. She makes an X beside the name. Raising her head, she says, Very good, you may be seated. She hears the geography lesson. Catherine Legrand is at the blackboard. Madame La Porte asks What is a river, what is a mountain, what is a sea? Catherine Legrand cannot answer these questions. Everybody has seen a river. It is a stream only bigger. Madame La Porte seems not to have heard this answer. It is a place where there is water. No, that's not right. It is water that flows, and a sea is water that doesn't flow. That's not right either. Madame La Porte tells Catherine Legrand that she does not know her geography lesson. She smiles. You can see all her teeth. She says that a river is a large body of water that flows into the sea, unlike a stream which is also a body of water but flows into a river. And a torrent? Can you tell me what a torrent is? It is a river near its source. No, not necessarily. Madame La Porte smiles again and says that a torrent is a mountainous body of water which is violent and whose rate of flow is irregular. She emphasizes the words violent and irregular. Catherine Legrand, can you tell me why a torrent has an irregular rate of flow? Catherine Legrand does not know what is meant by the rate of flow of a torrent, therefore she cannot possibly explain why it is irregular. Madame La Porte talks about the thawing of snow, glaciers, atmospheric precipitation, erosion. She pauses after each word. Then she acts as if she is taking a little breath, it is a sigh or a pant. She smiles. Catherine Legrand stands between Madame La Porte's chair and the blackboard waiting for Madame La Porte to finish talking. Madame La Porte is saying that you should have known all this for a long time, that after all it is only review. Reine Dieu raises her finger and before she has been given permission to speak she says in a very loud voice that Mademoiselle never hears their lessons. There is not a sound in the classroom. Everybody looks at Madame La Porte. She motions to Reine Dieu that she may be seated. She smiles at her. Is that so? But she does not wait for the answer. She turns back to Catherine Legrand who is still standing between Madame La Porte's chair and the blackboard. She seems not to hear Reine Dieu grumbling in a loud voice. She tells Catherine Legrand, I will give you a chance to redeem yourself by asking you another question. Can you tell me what a valley is? Of course Catherine Legrand has already noticed that the relief map contains both bumps and hollows. The valleys are the hollows. Madame La Porte begins to laugh. That's not it at all. Can someone answer me? Françoise Pommier raises her finger. Madame La Porte nods that she may speak. Françoise Pommier stands up beside the bench and speaks very rapidly. She says that a valley is a depression of either fluvial or glacial origin, that a fluvial valley is in the shape of a big V, while a glacial valley is more bell-shaped and is in the shape of a big U. All this while Madame La Porte is nodding her head to say yes, yes, yes, that's right. At the end she says out loud, That is very good I'm giving you a ten. Françoise Pommier waits for permission to sit back down. Everybody looks at her. Madame La Porte says to Catherine Legrand, I'm giving you zero, her lips go apart, you can see her pale pink gums, A nice big zero, and she smiles. And she makes a big zero in the notebook which she shows to Catherine Legrand. But it is not serious you may return to your seat. She gives her a little pat on the cheek. Madame La Porte is reading a story out loud. She has the book in front of her on the desk. Her hands are crossed one on top of the other. They uncross whenever one, the right one, has to turn the page. From time to time she shifts the book a little.

She looks up after almost every word and starts the next one and looks at the class and smiles. She looks first at the pupils sitting right in front of her, then at those on the right, then at those on the left. And she bows her head again and begins to read very slowly. Her lips rise very high above her teeth. You never lose sight of her pale pink gums. Madame La Porte's saliva flows freely. It clings to her teeth, it makes white strings which stick or stretch and stay for a moment on the lower lip then break like an elastic that is pulled too tight or too limp, leaving a fleck of white on the lip, a trace. It begins to make threads again each time the mouth closes and opens, each time the lips separate vertically or longitudinally. Madame La Porte has too much ptyalin. When she has finished reading the story she asks you to make up sentences, any sentences you like, as long as they have to do with what you just heard. Reine Dieu hasn't heard a word of the whole story. For this reason she has her arms folded on her notebook which remains blank. Madame La Porte reads out loud what Denise Baume and Anne-Marie Losserand have written in their notebooks. But instead of reading out loud what Catherine Legrand has written in her notebook Madame La Porte takes her in her arms, she carries Catherine Legrand in her arms bodily, a funny sight, a big girl like her being carried like a baby, Madame La Porte rocks her as she walks across the classroom, rocks her from side to side saying, My baby, my big baby, and smiling. Mademoiselle says that Anne-Marie

Losserand will not come to class because her little
brother is dead, she says that you will all go to see
him, she says that you will take flowers. Mademoiselle
says, you must not talk or move, you will kiss Anne-
Marie Losserand. You walk in line two by two. You
cross the square with the big traffic circle and the
bandstand in the middle. Everybody is noisy on the
stairs. There isn't enough room on the landing. Some
of you are standing on each step. You are still in twos.
You can't all go in at once. Mademoiselle divides the
class into two groups. The first group goes into Anne-
Marie Losserand's house with her, the other half remains on the landing overflowing down the stairs.
You jostle each other, you push each other down.
Mademoiselle yells to restore order. You follow her
into Anne-Marie Losserand's house. Anne-Marie Losserand's mother closes the door behind you. Anne-
Marie is beside her by the door. Neither of them is
crying. You go into the room where the little brother
is lying. He is a baby without any hair with his eyes
closed. It is just as if he had never opened them, like
little kittens that you don't want to keep. He is in his
cradle under a white net. Beside him on a little table
is a cross and the glass of holy water with the palm
inside. You make a circle in the room, walking on tiptoe. Mademoiselle begins in a low voice, Our Father
which art in heaven. When she has finished this she
goes on to the Hail Mary. You all join in at Holy
Mary Mother of God. Mademoiselle takes the palm
branch out of the holy water and makes the sign of

the cross over the cradle. She hands the palm branch to Françoise Pommier who is beside her. Françoise Pommier dips it in the holy water and you take turns making the sign of the cross over the cradle. You walk back and forth. You bump into each other. The room is not very big. But you don't make much noise. You see that Anne-Marie Losserand's mother has raised the net over the cradle. A thick mucus is coming out of the dead baby's nostrils. The mother wipes it with a handkerchief. She makes plugs out of absorbent cotton and stuffs them into the baby's nostrils to stop them up. When she has finished she lowers the net veil. You back out of the room. As you leave you look at the dead baby lying under the veil of white net with the cotton coming out of his nose. You make way for the other half of the class. You wait on the landing. You jostle each other. You whisper. You sit on the steps of the staircase. You hear Mademoiselle saying the Our Father and the Hail Mary in a low voice. The ground is damp and almost black. Chestnut blossoms have fallen in the night. You can see little red lines on the inside of each fluttering blossom they look like snow against the black of the ground. Véronique Legrand and Catherine Legrand are in the garden. Véronique Legrand is pestering Monsieur Ponse. She says to him, Monsieur Ponse, Monsieur Ponse, you can't catch me. He is in front of his workbench. There are lots of tools, some hanging from the wall, others lying on the workbench, there are wood saws, hacksaws, circular saws, there are compass saws

of various sizes, wood files, metal files, a pair of cali-
pers, there is a hand drill, there are awls of all sorts
and sizes. There are also nails, screws, glue, and above
all big blocks of wood. Véronique Legrand touches all
these things. She holds the hammers in her hand to
feel their weight. She closes and opens the vise. She
fingers the nails, she scoops them up in handfuls and
drops them again. She starts to nail a row of little
nails to the top of the workbench. She hits them with
the hammer, holding it by the head for added strength.
Monsieur Ponse is carving a monster out of the block
of wood he is holding between his knees. Painstak-
ingly he cuts scales into the surface to make the back.
Catherine Legrand tries to climb up the rope of the
swing. She uses her legs and feet to pull herself up
the rope which is not stout enough to provide a firm
grip. She falls back onto the seat again and again. The
swing is between two big lime trees. When you stand
up to make it swing and lean back you can see the sky
between the two trees. You go into the orchard to
gather apples. There are salad greens planted in separate plots of ground. Lettuce, escarole. There are also
a few clumps of parsley here and there and some
sprigs of thyme. You have permission to gather the
apples that have fallen in the night. Sometimes these
are apples which have started to go bad on the tree
and you can't tell right away. They are lying with
the rotten part toward the grass, it is brown, it is
buried in the grass, it is hidden. You pick up the apple
because you only see the whole side which is pale

green, sometimes pink, sometimes red, then your fingers sink into the rotten part. Some of the apples fall because they are infested with larvae. They do not remain on the tree until they are ripe. The larva has made tunnels in the fruit, it has mined it. The apple has lost its solidity. It is half-gutted. It falls. The good apples stay on the tree. They aren't allowed to touch them because they're not ripe. If you shake the tree just a tiny bit harder than the wind one or two apples may fall, and their stems show a fresh, green break. Véronique Legrand scoops out the apples she finds under the trees with a piece of scrap iron. She enlarges the tunnels made by the larvae so that they cave in. She lines up the apples she has worked on against the house on the side with the blank wall. Some still have shreds of green skin. From time to time Véronique Legrand munches one absent-mindedly or to see how it tastes. On the ground by the house she draws a kind of rectangle marking off her domain with the piece of scrap iron she has in her hand. In the rectangle she stores the apples she is working on. After a moment the ants attack them. Some are completely covered with ants. Véronique Legrand drops the hollow apples which she is carrying off in her arms and starts to run screaming, Ant's nest, ant's nest. When you have several empty cans you can use them to soak all kinds of leaves in water. You make mixtures: lilac, nettles, apple leaves. In certain cans you soak only flower petals: rose, tulip, peony, to obtain essences. You put them in the sun and every so often you stir them with a stick. After a few hours the water is warm and the liquid has a smell. But leaves and petals are hard to dissolve. No matter how careful you are the liquid has a rotten smell. But if you keep on, if you sniff for a while eventually you can distinguish the good smell—apple, rose, or tulip, as the case may be. You take the cans into Véronique Legrand's rectangle. Véronique Legrand is making walls to protect her acquisitions from the elements. It takes a long time. You have to transfer all the stones you find at each end of the garden to Véronique Legrand's rectangle. You have to sort them and put them in order of size. The base of the wall is made up of the biggest and flattest stones. It gets narrower as it goes up because there aren't many big stones. The wall stops growing when you run out of them. To finish it off on top you pile little stones or pebbles which don't look anything like building stones and which spoil the whole effect. Since you have nothing to cement the different kinds of stone together with, the walls aren't solid. You're always having to repair them. Véronique Legrand has her hands full. When you get one wall in good condition, another collapses. You've tried to put them together in a more permanent fashion with very damp red earth. You pretend it's potter's clay. But when it dries it crumbles, it doesn't hold, it doesn't stay between the stones, the stones come apart, get crooked and fall down, and when one falls it sets off a chain reaction and the whole thing is pulled down with it, stone by stone. Beside a group

73

of adult trees are some shrubs with straight and slender trunks. They are in twos and threes. They don't give any shade and this allows the growth of eglantine and a tangle of bushes of all kinds that come halfway up their trunks. They are taller than little girls, though, so this is Catherine Legrand's and Véronique Legrand's forest. Here you learn to climb trees. You hold the trunk between your arms and thighs and pull yourself up with all your might. You bark your skin. You can't get all the way to the top. You stop, you can't move another inch. The muscles in your thighs and arms have ceased to obey. You wait for a minute, you rest. You try to forget that you are tired by watching the top leaves and the sky moving across them. You try to move again. But it is impossible. All you can do is slide down the trunk until you touch the ground. You get caught on knots and shoots on the way. When you get to the bottom your legs are bloody. You hang from a branch by your hands. You swing your body back and forth to work up momentum and then you heave it suddenly onto the branch. You rock your body back and forth. At first very gently then harder and harder. Finally it rocks so hard back and forth that your hands lose their grip and you fall face down into the nettles, bare arms, bare legs, bare thighs. At first you don't feel anything. You're dazed by the fall. When you realize that you are in the nettles you get up as fast as you can but it's too late, the blood begins to run all over, it stings, you feel it moving very fast around your

74

neck on your arms on your thighs you are pricked dotted by the needles which are under the leaves and along the stalk of the nettle and when you look you are already covered with blisters. Mademoiselle is kneeling at her prie-dieu in the middle of the aisle. The whole class is beside her in the pews. You are at mass. Catherine Legrand is next to Reine Dieu. You are sitting down. The priest has not arrived. Reine Dieu has some religious pictures made of some kind of cloth, there is lace around the edges like on the chrisom cloth for the altar. You run your fingers over it. The scallops move like the cloth of a flag when someone is waving it. Reine Dieu brings the picture close to her eyes and looks through the holes of the lace at Catherine Legrand. As she does this she pulls her mouth first to the right then to the left, baring her teeth and gums. From where she is Mademoiselle can only watch two rows of pupils. You are some-where behind her. The priest arrives in his surplice. He goes to the foot of the altar. He kneels and says, *In nomine patris et filii et,* making the sign of the cross. Mademoiselle makes the sign of the cross too almost at the same time he does, beginning with the forehead and going to the chest. You say Amen with Mademoiselle. The priest says, *Introibo ad altare Dei.* After that you don't understand anything. Reine Dieu drops one of the two candies you are about to eat under the pew. You have a terrible time getting it back. First Reine Dieu slips under the pew in front and scrambles around between Pascale Delaroche's and

Jacqueline Marchand's legs, and you can hear her getting kicked and defending herself with her fists. She comes up without the candy and searches under the pews in back. She crawls under them backwards. Catherine Legrand taps her on the head to warn her. Mademoiselle has turned around twice but she hasn't seen anything after all. Reine Dieu reappears just as you are sitting down. She hasn't found it. Catherine Legrand who is shorter and thinner tries too. She looks all around, in all the corners where Reine Dieu didn't go. She is very quiet. Nobody notices she is there, so that she doesn't get kicked. After a moment of crawling on all fours she puts her hand on something hard and brings up stuck to her palm a sticky raspberry candy covered with dust. Reine Dieu tells her she can keep it and swallows the other. You try to push each other off the pew so quietly that Mademoiselle doesn't hear a sound. You look at each other out of the corner of your eye and take aim then you shove with your shoulder. Suddenly Reine Dieu who is on the end of the pew tumbles into the aisle. You hear her hands smack against the tiles as she hits the floor. Mademoiselle hasn't heard anything. You sit still for a minute. You see that Mademoiselle isn't turning around. Very carefully you remove Pascale Delaroche's beret, her hair stands up as you do so. Pascale Delaroche puts her hand on her head and finds that her beret is gone. She whirls around and grabs Catherine Legrand to get it back. You wrestle, you scuffle, you grab each other by the chest and shoulders but it doesn't really make any noise. Catherine Legrand manages to pass Pascale Delaroche's beret under her arm to Reine Dieu who passes it behind her to Denise Baume. You hear a bell ring three times. In front of the altar a boy in a red robe and a white lace surplice is ringing a little bell, it is the elevation. Mademoiselle turns around to see whether every head is bowed. Everyone puts her head against her chest. After a moment you raise your head. The choir boy has on beige wool socks and high brown shoes. One of his shoelaces is untied. The red robe comes just below his knees. He rings three more times and you bow your head again. When the elevation is over Denise Baume throws Pascale Delaroche's beret over Reine Dieu's head and it lands in the middle of the aisle just behind Mademoiselle. Pascale Delaroche is all red. She doesn't want to go and get her beret where it is, she shakes Catherine Legrand to make her go instead, You're the one who took it. She tries to take Catherine Legrand's beret. In the end Catherine Legrand marches right up and gets it. She walks back to her seat without Mademoiselle noticing. Then she returns the beret to Pascale Delaroche. You hear the priest say, *Agnus Dei qui tollis peccata mundi*. Catherine Legrand realizes that mass is almost over and she hasn't prayed yet. She puts her head in her hands. The balls of her fingers press against her closed eyelids. You watch all the orange and blue circles and all the yellow stripes that live between your eyes and your eyelids go by. You ask His pardon for playing all

77

through mass. For a moment you love Him with all your might. You look at the altar between your spread fingers. The priest is administering communion. You keep your head in your hands for a very long moment. You hear the priest say, *Ite missa est*, you say with Mademoiselle, *Deo gratias*. More time goes by. Reine Dieu says, That's the last gospels. And you make the last sign of the cross. Mademoiselle gets up. Françoise Pommier gets up from the pews to put away her prie-dieu. Mademoiselle claps her hands. You are standing in front of the pews. You file out two by two, genuflecting as you pass the altar. Whenever Reine Dieu does it she puts her leg so far back that she almost falls flat on her face. The river has overflowed. The water comes clear to the middle of the garden. Two fields are completely covered with it. Father makes marks with wooden pickets to measure the rise of the water. It is still raining. Even the fields on the other side of the road are hidden by sheets of water. It is because the ground is completely saturated that the water remains on the surface. It freezes in the night. The sheets of water are transformed into blocks of ice. Now there are skating rinks all over the fields. You go under the barbed-wire fences. You go for slides with your satchel under your arm. You push each other to go faster. You slide sideways with your right foot forward. When you can take a head start you end up crouching dragging the satchel along the ice. Reine Dieu and Catherine Legrand take Véronique Legrand by the hand and

78

run pulling her crouching between them the length of the skating rink. Jennie Tellier falls down and cuts her forehead. You can see the blood on the ice. She puts a handkerchief to it. It gets red right away. Denise Baume goes home with her. You are going to explore the fields of ice. You go under a lot of barbed-wire fences. Reine Dieu tears her coat on a barb. There are piles of ice, some with smooth surfaces others in broken blocks, some are stuck straight into the ground like rocks. You jump from one to the other being careful because it's slippery. Catherine Legrand loses a shoe between two blocks. The others don't stop. Everyone is already far away. Catherine Legrand and Véronique Legrand stay behind all alone. Catherine Legrand sits on the ice and tries to get hold of the shoe. She can't do it. She has to slide the length of one of the blocks. The shoe is wedged underneath. Véronique Legrand stands beside her in the field and watches her. It is almost dark. Catherine Legrand manages to get her shoe out and slips it on over her soaked and muddy woolen anklet. There is no more sunlight. Night will fall in another moment. It is starting to get cold. Their clothes are all wet and stick to their bodies. The flat card houses are quite near now. To get back home you have to go back across all the fields, under all the barbed-wire fences. Catherine Legrand lifts them up one after the other so Véronique Legrand can go under them. You hold hands on the national highway. You put all your clothes on the porch in front of the boiler of the

79

central heating system to dry. They make a thick steam which smells of dampness and overheated wool. The red reflector sways and shines on the back of the bicycle and moves with the zigzags and turns made by the invisible cyclist on the seat. The bicycle seems to stay in the same place. At times you could swear that the red reflector is higher, that it is several meters above the ground, that now it doesn't move and that it is zigzagging toward Catherine Legrand alone on the road. The wooden fences and wire netting by the roadside are shapeless masses. The houses are far behind somewhere. Between the fences and them, between Catherine Legrand and them there is a desert which the road is part of and where the bicycle reflector wavers fuzzy and red. You went into the forest this afternoon. You found periwinkles and jonquils. You made them into bouquets which you stuck in your belt so you could keep on running more easily. You ate lunch in a clearing. You sat in a circle. Mademoiselle leaned against the trunk of a beech tree. You drew straws to see who would tell a story. You cut pieces of wood into sticks which were all the same length except one. Mademoiselle held them in her hand in a bunch so all the ends were even. You took turns picking sticks. Anne-Marie Losserand drew the one that was shorter than the others. She told the story of a princess who is mistreated by her stepmother and stepsisters. These women are wicked and ugly. The princess is beautiful and good. The princess is not allowed to go to the ball. But she puts a chicken wing on her head, an onion peel around her neck she puts on the cook's apron and waits in her room for the fairy to come and fix everything with her wand make the chicken feather beautiful and iron the apron. Anne-Marie Losserand's story is very long. Mademoiselle smiles and nods her head as she listens. The undergrowth gets darker. Mademoiselle tells Anne-Marie Losserand that she may finish her story tomorrow in class that they must leave right away or they will not be home before dark. You get up. You throw away the bouquets you have in your belt, the stems are broken and the flowers with their drooping heads are useless. At the foot of the beech tree Catherine Legrand leaves the silk scarf that her mother lent her on the condition that she not lose it. You are in the playground. It is already completely dark except for a dim glow where the sun went down. Catherine Legrand suddenly remembers that she left the scarf under the beech tree. She wants to go back right now. She says she won't get lost that she knows the way very well. Mademoiselle doesn't want Catherine Legrand to go alone into the forest at night. Catherine Legrand says, I will take Reine Dieu, we know the way. Reine Dieu says, Yes yes let's go. Mademoiselle says, I forbid you. Mademoiselle says that there is a ghost in the forest, that it is very foolish to go there now because he is there at night and that if Reine Dieu and Catherine Legrand go there they will die. No one knows what a ghost is. You ask Mademoiselle what a ghost is. She says it is a dead person who leaves his grave, that you can tell he is a ghost because he has his shroud over his head, that he waits for people and sucks blood from their throats. You laugh. But you aren't very sure that Mademoiselle is joking. You ask her if it is true. She says it is. She says she would never go into Saints' Forest at night because of the ghost. You ask her how she knows this. She says that a gentleman she knows has seen it. But then the ghost didn't suck his blood? No, he managed to escape because he was a man and because he didn't lose his self-control. And what does the ghost do when there is nobody in the forest? He waits for someone to come. And what if nobody goes there? He keeps on waiting. Probably he has plenty of time. Reine Dieu says in Catherine Legrand's ear, That's a lot of shit we're going anyway. You don't dare talk too loud on the road. You say goodbye without mentioning the forest again. Reine Dieu has turned left to go toward the church. Catherine Legrand keeps on straight ahead until she comes to the national highway where she turns right. Ahead on the road the reflector moves like the lamps divers hold in their hands in stories. What if it weren't a reflector at all? What if it were the red lamp of the altar in the hand of a dead person? Of course you don't have to believe in that ghost business; but even so Mademoiselle really tells it that way, as if it were true, as if she were really afraid of them. Catherine Legrand stops in the road. There isn't any other way to get home. You have to go straight ahead it's the only thing to do you have to brave it since behind you all the doors of the school are closed there isn't anybody left on the playground or in the classroom now. Catherine Legrand starts to run to get it over with sooner. The road is all dark. You manage to cheer yourself up with the thought of the two street lamps which you come to as soon as you turn off the road onto the national highway. In just a few moments you'll be there, in the zone of light. Catherine Legrand runs by an old man on a bicycle who sways on the seat and pedals so slowly that it must be so as not to lose his balance because he looks as if he isn't moving, you can only see the front wheel turning now to the left now to the right depending on which way the old man leans on the handlebars. Mother says, What's all this about a ghost? She knits her brow as she does when Catherine Legrand tells a lie, You must have misunderstood, there are no such things as ghosts, that's what you heard, you can't possibly have heard the opposite, think about it a little and you'll see that ghosts do not exist. Fine, that's what Mother says. But Mademoiselle nodded her head and rolled her eyes up and down and to the sides meaning yes it is true there are ghosts in the forests. So in the end you have no idea what ghosts are and whether they exist or not. Mademoiselle is standing in front of the door to the classroom talking with Fabienne Dires's mother. Fabienne Dires's mother is short she has a navy blue coat on she has short hair. You can't see her very well because Mademoiselle is in the way. Inside the classroom you are having fun.

You are throwing erasers at each other. Reine Dieu hurls hers so hard against a windowpane that everybody puts their heads down on their desks because they really believe it is about to break into a thousand pieces. It doesn't break. Mademoiselle turns around and says, Will you sit still? Denise Baume turns halfway around on the bench so that Pascale Delaroche sitting beside her and Reine Dieu and Catherine Legrand behind her can hear what she is saying. She says that she went to Aunt's house to visit. You go there in a car. You have to cross the border. There is a lake. The houses are all white and you can see swans on the water they are all white too except for one with a black spot on his neck. You throw them crumbs. Aunt gave Denise Baume a mechanical bear with red trousers who dances and beats a drum when you wind him up in back. Everyone is happy. Aunt has made a huge cake with designs on it. On the way back you go through a pass with a funny name, The Collar. A pass is the highest part of the mountain, the last part that you can see. It is located at the neck of the mountain. This is why you call it a collar. You can't see the head because it is in the clouds. From the collar you look down and see the whole lake like on a map, you can see high mountains even Mont Blanc, you can see parts of two countries and maybe a third between the mountains, Poland. Denise Baume loves to travel. You eat in restaurants at noon and night. There is a dog who comes and sits beside your chair and you feed him out of your hand. The dog stays there and every time you take a bite his ears prick up and he stands very stiff on his feet. Mademoiselle turns around and begins yelling, Be quiet. She can't hear what Fabienne Dires's mother is saying to her. By the time you begin to understand what she said she has already resumed her conversation. Fabienne Dires's mother is moving sideways toward the embrasure of the door. Mademoiselle is following her step by step and trying not to lose ground. Pascale Delaroche has turned halfway around on the bench and is talking to Denise Baume who sits beside her and at the same time to Reine Dieu and Catherine Legrand who sit behind her. She says, My little brother believes sure as shooting that if he does it right, by running back and forth in the big room and beating his arms very fast he will be able to take off. Pascale Delaroche raises and lowers her forearms very fast, her behind sticking out like a big hen or a duck, Pascale Delaroche sitting on her bench really looks as if she were about to fly away any minute. You laugh. Catherine Legrand wiggles beside Reine Dieu. Denise Baume Pascale Delaroche Reine Dieu look at her. Catherine Legrand takes off her shoe pulling on the laces. Denise Baume Pascale Delaroche Reine Dieu look at her. Catherine Legrand tears off her wool sock and puts her foot on the desk bare as a bean you can see her toenails the toes spread it's hard to keep your foot in this position a foot which may not be too clean either Catherine Legrand didn't think of that she did it to make Denise Baume Pascale Delaroche Reine Dieu laugh but nobody is laughing. Each little girl turns back to her desk as if to begin working. Nobody speaks. Nobody looks at Catherine Legrand. Catherine Legrand is putting her sock and shoe back on. Perhaps it wasn't funny and this is why something starts to whirl inside of what seems to be Catherine Legrand and by the time Catherine Legrand has finished lacing her shoe it's very heavy inside her, it hovers in back of her eyes, it looks out through the sockets, it's caught, it can never be anything else but Catherine Legrand. It is good to walk in the meadows in summer. Mademoiselle points to each tree with her finger and says that you are going to learn about nature. You must be able to recognize apple trees, plum trees, cherry trees, you must learn to distinguish oats from barley and wheat. The trunk of an apple tree has bark with deep grooves that run parallel to each other from top to bottom. The bark looks like a plowed field in autumn when the earth is brown. It is the same color. You have an apple tree in front of you that is a big and old tree. It has two main branches which form a fork in which you could lie. Mademoiselle forbids you to climb trees. In the grooves of its bark there are ants swarming sometimes you see a whole row of them. The leaves of the apple tree are round and dull. They have a downy look especially on the underside it looks as if there is a layer of white over the green it's so milky. Mademoiselle says that the blossoms of the apple tree are pink. Plum trees are less solid-looking. The trunk of the plum tree is glossier almost black full of knots and gashlike things running up and down, its branches diverge and even the stoutest ones end in supple shoots that bend. The forks, which are not the result of real overlapping, do not provide stable shelters. Mademoiselle says that the blossoms of the plum tree are white. Pear trees have elongated leaves that are a silvery green color. The trunks are as gnarled and pitted as those of apple trees. Mademoiselle says that the blossoms of the pear tree are white. The most beautiful of these kinds of trees are the cherry trees, especially those that bear bigaroons. They are very straight their trunks are not very thick these trees remind you of horses because you feel as if there were blood racing beneath the bark. You can't believe that they will stay quietly planted in the ground like this for long. Their bark is smooth and silky like that of birch trees. It is pearl gray. The forks, the bases of new branches, the overall pattern of the branches, the way they are put together never has anything sloppy about it. It seems planned and right. They form arches that stand out against the sky like a colonnade in a French-style garden, they spring up stiffly, they are geometric, the leaves are shiny green but dark they are not very long they are not very narrow they have fine notches around the edges. Mademoiselle says that the blossoms of the cherry tree are white. As a matter of fact you have already seen them in the garden in the springtime. The petals are on the black ground and the wet trunk is the same color. You gather them. The tips of your fingers are wet. There are some around the tree. There are some on the leafless branches where they form white clusters, drooping snowy heaps. It is even easier to tell the grains apart. Ears of barley are tapered like ears of wheat but they have long fine beards, they are narrower than wheat and less heavy. Ears of oats are plumed. They look like a swarm in which the insects always hover the same distance apart. The grains are encased in pale-green sheaths with beards at the end. The fields of graminaceous plants are bordered with hedged paths where you feel as if you were walking in the shade. The grass is full of colors. The pinks of the tops of graminaceous plants are very pale almost transparent. There are some that look like oats, some have downy tufts, others have ears. Grass is not included in the nature lesson. When you walk in it it comes up high. You try to walk without leaving a trace. But when you turn around and look behind you it looks as if you had slashed the field with a knife. And then you see the yellow dots of buttercups and dandelions forming patches here and there as if sunlight were scattered over the meadow. You enter a little patch of forest by pushing open a fence made of pickets which have been loosely joined with barbed wire. Reine Dieu says the hairs that are caught in the barbs are from a wild boar. You can see very well that he lost them by going by too fast or by trying too hard to pass or because he didn't see the fence. Reine Dieu says that actually wild boars are almost blind. The hairs that you try to pluck from the places where the wire is twisted together are very stiff and black. You tell yourself that you would like to see a wild boar. Reine Dieu says that they hardly ever come out of the dense undergrowth, the thickets where they make their lairs. It is hot. You can't take another step. You are perspiring. Your cheeks are red. Your cheeks are purple. You think of mint, green and ice-cold. You think of spring water. You think of pebbles, all small, white and cool. There isn't any water anywhere. You don't hear any springs. You are walking unprotected on a tar road. When you see the inviting shade of a tree or the wall of a house you stop and rest in it to cool off. This isn't easy because right now the shadows are short and hot. There is a little girl who has a hole in her palate. Catherine Legrand is beside her at Evening Service. Mademoiselle took her by the hand and showed her to a pew saying that she is a new pupil, that you must be nice to her, that she is sick, that she has a hole in her palate. Then everybody wanted to see the hole and Mademoiselle made her open her mouth. Everybody crowded around her. Catherine Legrand thought she saw something yellow and black in the middle of the palate but Catherine Legrand can't swear that she has seen the hole in the new girl's palate. When Mademoiselle asked, Who will look after her on the way to Evening Service, Reine Dieu and Catherine Legrand both said, Me, because of the hole in her palate. The monstrance is on the altar. The priest is kneeling in front of it in a white surplice which is scalloped at the bottom. The monstrance is made of gold. It is a sun whose rays are frozen in the shape of a torso. The round part of the sun is the host. The little girl with the hole in her palate is kneeling between Reine Dieu and Catherine Legrand. She is always opening her mouth it seems as if she opens it every time she takes a breath sometimes her mouth stays open for a while. Catherine Legrand believes that this is when a smell of rot or diarrhea or something worse that Catherine Legrand can't identify comes out of her mouth. It is better to turn your head the other way. When the little girl closes her mouth you don't smell it any more. Reine Dieu looks in front of her. She drops her rosary under the pew. She has trouble finding it because it is under the third pew back. She crawls backward under the pews. The pupils in the higher grades hit her with their feet, knees and fists, when she gets it back she begins to untangle it. You can't tell whether the smell really comes from the little girl with the hole in her palate or if you're only imagining it maybe it's a dog or cat that came in during the day when the doors of the church are wide open and went to the bathroom there under the pew. You have seen dogs come into church during service and trot up to the choir. You start to laugh when this happens. Especially when the dog stops and doesn't know what to do next and wags his tail. You have also seen swallows fly right under the dome, fly right by and graze the cornerstones, the supports, from down below they look as if they will bump into them but they keep on flying they swerve at the last moment you watch them with your head way back, you lean on the nape of your neck to see them as long as possible especially when they fly the other way toward the door, you wonder whether they can fly backwards or with their feet in the air. It is Thursday afternoon at Fabienne Dires's house. You are playing theater. The stage is the garden. Everybody is on stage. Fabienne Dires's little brother plays the little boy. Fabienne Dires plays the little boy's mother. Denise Baume plays the little boy's mother's neighbor. Véronique Legrand plays the little boy's mother's doctor. Catherine Legrand plays the little boy's mother's priest. It is time to go to school. The little boy falls flat on his face on the ground just as the mother sets him on his feet. You have a lot of trouble making Fabienne Dires's little brother fall to the ground properly. He stands stiffly, it looks as if he is falling several times this is because he is holding himself back. You explain to him that he must fall flat on his face right away. To show him the right way to do it Catherine Legrand trips him. As a result Fabienne Dires's little brother falls flat on his face on the ground just as you want him to but his forehead hits the root of a tree and he begins to cry. In the end you make him fall on a plot of grass and it works pretty well. Now there is no way to make him stop falling down. The mother of the little boy who falls down goes to get the neighbor and sets him on his feet in front of her to show her how he can't stay that way. Just then the little brother is supposed to fall flat on his face. The mother picks him up again and sets him on his feet in front of the priest. He can't stop falling down. No matter how many times you set him on his feet he falls down and nobody knows why. The mother picks him up again and sets him on his feet in front of the doctor. The doctor says, Don't cry Madame, I'll fix him up and he asks to listen to his heart and this is how he notices that when he got dressed he put both feet into the same trouser leg. You pull the curtain and the actors applaud themselves but do not call Encore. Reine Dieu is drawing a maze on the ground. She says that once you get inside it you can't get out again. Everybody gets inside it. You take very small steps to find the way out. Fabienne Dires's little brother cheats he jumps over the lines and says, I've won. You tell him that if that's how he acts you won't play with him any more. You start all over again. You go back to the beginning of the maze. Anne-Marie Losserand tells Reine Dieu that her maze isn't right because there are lines that cross other lines and that's not fair. Reine Dieu tries to fix some of the lines but she throws down her stick and says that there isn't enough room to make a real maze. You decide to erase it and start another one including the lawn and using little white pebbles placed very close together to make the lines that must go through the grass. Fabienne Dires's little brother kicks the pebbles as soon as you put them on the grass. Reine Dieu Fabienne Dires Véronique Legrand Catherine Legrand Denise Baume run after him. When you catch him you make him sit on top of a wall which he can't get down from by himself and he starts to cry and kick his feet against the wall. You show Reine Dieu's maze to two little girls you don't know. Fabienne Dires's mother tells them to come inside that it is time for tea. Fabienne Dires is talking to the two strange little girls. She calls the bigger one Françoise and the smaller one Jacqueline. In the house it smells of cinnamon and lemon tart. You take off your coats. You put them back on to go outside after tea. The bigger of the little girls the one whose name is Françoise suggests that you see who can jump highest against the wall. She shows how you do it she throws up her leg and so reaches the top of the wall. When she does this you can see her vulva her buttocks and the crack between them because her panties are all torn. You tell her to do it again so you can see. When she turns around laughing and sees the looks on your faces she gets all red and you can't talk her into jumping up the wall again. Since the beginning of the history lesson Mademoiselle has been talking about Charlemagne who became emperor in the year 800. Mademoiselle says that Charlemagne founded schools, she says that in the school in his palace the children of the poor could go with the children of the rich. In the color plate in the history book you see Charlemagne standing there in a robe with his arm around a child of the poor and this child has a scroll in his hand and he is looking up at Charlemagne maybe he is talking to him. You can tell he is a child of the poor because the hem of his robe is uneven. Charlemagne is shaking the index finger of the hand that is not around the child of the poor at a child of the rich whose robe has a straight hem, Mademoiselle says he looks mad, she says Charlemagne is scolding him and asking why it is that a child of the poor works harder than he. Behind Charlemagne you can see rows of other children that get smaller and smaller. There aren't any little girls in the picture. Mademoiselle says you can't see it in the picture but Charlemagne made war on the Saxons who had a leader named Witikind. Mademoiselle says Witikind was beaten by Charlemagne in this war and that Charlemagne wanted Witikind to become a Christian but Witikind didn't want to. But Mademoiselle says that one day he went to church all alone and there he saw a little child in the host of the monstrance and that he fell on his knees and became a Christian. Mademoiselle says that in Avignon the sun is always shining and the sky is always blue. She looks out the window but you can see that it is raining. During the geography lesson she says that a great wind swoops down on the valley of the Rhone as if it were a corridor and blows the white and pink flowers off the peach and almond trees and that during all this the sky stays blue. She says that beside the fields there are straight rows of cypress and yew trees to protect the crops from the wind and they are dark green and they grow in the direction of the wind from being pushed in that direction. Mademoiselle takes off her glasses and says that this is the mistral.

You have put the gun in the middle. If anyone came from Catherine Legrand's left or Vincent Parme's right he couldn't see it, one of them could just walk back and forth in front of the barrel of the gun as he talked and meanwhile the other could grab it and hide it behind his back. You are walking along the river. You are stooping. You move at a crouch. When it is completely dark nobody will be able to see you except for Vincent Parme's white shirt. You fall flat on your face in the grass because the mill girls are walking over the wooden plank and coming on the bad side, instead of going upstream on the other side of the mill dam and following the branch of the river that has been deflected across the field as far as the mill, they are going downstream, which means that they are coming toward you. They are turning their backs on their house. When they go home they will say that they have seen Vincent Parme and Catherine Legrand lying in the field on either side of the gun. For the moment you are hidden by the base of a hazel tree which grows right beside the water and spreads far over the meadow. The grass is damp. The ground is damp. You hear the sound the water makes as it flows right by. It is like when you're lying in bed at night and can't go to sleep. In the daytime you don't hear anything at all. The mill girls are tall and very thin. You don't play with them. They bend over to pick up or look at something you can't see in the meadow. When they have finished they go toward the mill, they cut across the field. They don't look in your direction. They turn their backs. You wait until they have gone into the house. You continue walking along the river. You pass the hazel tree. Vincent Parme is holding the gun. This time he has it on the river side. You stop in front of the wooden plank. Vincent Parme throws the gun into the grass. In the part that overhangs the bank you make holes in the ground, as round and neat as possible. You make six in all, rather far apart. When you have finished digging you can see the water of the river through the holes. It eats deep under the bank around here.

From your pocket you take a piece of wire in which you have made a slipknot. You slip the end of the wire into the knot so as to make a loop which is half flexible and half rigid. After the loop you still have a bit of wire left over which you take in your hand. You squat beside the hole. You wait. When a trout stops there you plunge the loop into the water as quietly as you can and catch the trout's tail without touching it, you slide it up along his stomach and when you come to the gills you give a sharp tug and pull the trout out into the grass caught tightly in the wire. Catherine Legrand is watching three holes. Vincent Parme is watching three holes. It is almost dark. The river is lighter than the field. There is sunlight in the stream. A trout stops at the mouth of one of Vincent Parme's holes. Vincent Parme sticks the loop into the hole and gives a sharp tug to land the trout. It flops onto the grass first on one side then on the other. You can see its scales glisten. It lies still for a moment then starts to flop again for quite a while. A trout has stopped in one of Catherine Legrand's holes. Catherine Legrand sticks the wire in, the tail is in the loop, Catherine Legrand slides the wire along the stomach, the trout feels it and quickly slips away. Catherine Legrand doesn't see it again. She tells Vincent Parme that she has just lost a trout. Vincent Parme says that it doesn't matter, that it's just one of those things and there are plenty of them. The trout that Vincent Parme has caught makes a great leap in the grass and falls back on its side. Vincent Parme is pulling out a trout. It is too small he throws it back into the water. You can hear the noise it makes somewhere in the middle of the river. Vincent Parme tells Catherine Legrand to come and help him. He has trapped one in the hole closest to the water's edge. It is so big that he can't get it out through the hole. The trout is struggling. Vincent Parme lies flat on his belly and leans over the bank. He tries to land it this way. He tells Catherine Legrand to hold his feet. Catherine Legrand holds Vincent Parme's feet his whole body is leaning over the river. It is hard for Catherine Legrand to hold onto them because he is pulling on them the whole time. Suddenly you hear Aunt calling from the other side of the river, standing in the circle of the door light because it is time for dinner. Vincent Parme says Shit, as he lands the struggling trout. Catherine Legrand is holding his feet. Vincent Parme braces up and crawls back on his belly. He is sitting on the ground. In both hands he holds the trout which is struggling half caught in the wire and Vincent Parme's hands. It is a big trout. He puts it inside his shirt against his chest with the other one. You walk back along the river. You turn your back on the wooden plank which the mill girls walked over a little while ago. You take the wooden bridge whose slats bounce under your feet instead. Catherine Legrand carries the gun in her hand resting the barrel against her leg. It is all cold and wet. Vincent Parme walks holding the trout against his chest. You are very careful not to be seen by anybody because you aren't allowed to do this. You are up to your waist in sawdust. There are four of you in the same pile. You are playing cards. Denise Parme keeps winning. Vincent Parme is sulking. Véronique Legrand is buried almost up to her neck. The workshop isn't lighted. It is raining outdoors. The grass in the field is a darker shade of green than usual. You see that the outside trees of the forest are all weighed down. Véronique Legrand loses a card in the sawdust. When she looks for it she buries all the others. Catherine Legrand who is next to her digs holes to find the cards. She throws a lot of sawdust into Denise Parme's face. Denise Parme takes handfuls of sawdust and throws them at Catherine Legrand. You start to fight with the sawdust. You have a hard time getting out of it. You stand up and take aim at each other. Véronique Legrand screams because in trying to get out of it she is getting buried deeper and deeper. All the sawdust thrown by Vincent Parme lands in her face. At last she manages to get out. You throw sawdust all over the workshop your hair and pockets are full of it. You decide to go and steal apples while it isn't raining so hard. Denise Parme says they aren't ripe. You go anyway. The road runs along the forest. It is not a paved road. It has puddles and mud all over. To the right are the fields. To get to the apple trees you have to leave the road and walk through the grass for a while. On the first apple tree you see that the apples are very little, on the second they are the same. You find one that has regular apples. You stand underneath and Vincent

Parme shakes the branches with all his might. You run away screaming because of all the water that falls on you. Not a single apple falls. Denise Parme says that she told you they weren't ripe. Then you climb the tree to pick them. The trunk is all sticky. The soles of your shoes slip on the bark. When your pockets are full you climb back down. You are under the tree. You stamp on the ground. It is sodden. It makes a sucking noise under your feet, the grass looks like compost all over the meadow. You divide the apples. You throw away the greenest ones but you take as many as you can. You go back to the workshop. You are cold because you are soaked to the skin. You get in the pile of sawdust again. You each have your apples in front of you. You munch them as you play cards. Véronique Legrand takes a little bite out of each apple to taste it. She decides that the first is the one she will eat. The bitten part is full of sawdust because of the saliva and apple juice. Véronique Legrand has to rub it against her for quite a while and lick it clean before she can start to eat it. You eat and eat. Aunt calls you to tea. You run in yelling at the first one in. Aunt gets angry because of all the sawdust you bring into her house which she has just waxed. So you go back to the workshop. After a few minutes you have a stomach-ache. You leave the sawdust and run to get to the toilet before the others. Denise Parme gets there first and throws the bolt as fast as she can holding the door shut. Vincent Parme Catherine Legrand arrive immediately after. Véronique Legrand walks across the yard holding her stomach in her hands. Vincent Parme Catherine Legrand Véronique Legrand begin to drum on the door. Catherine Legrand and Véronique Legrand are taking the high road to the farm. It goes through the whole village at the place where some of the houses overhang the others. You can also get there by another road. This is the road where Catherine Legrand and Véronique Legrand get attacked. In the first place there are the geese. They are in a yard off the road, there is a fountain in the middle you don't see them right away because of the angle of the fountain or more often because an abandoned cart with its pole raised or even a manure pile gets in the way. Anyway, even when you think they aren't there they come running hobbling from one foot to the other, hastily shifting from one foot to the other the plumpness of their legs, feathers, flanks and down, their necks taut, their beaks gaping, jammed together honking and hissing your only choice is to pounce on them and yell louder than they do to scare them, they hardly flinch and run forward honking even louder than before. You pretend to kick them. They swerve to the side making a kind of croaking noise, but as soon as you turn your back to run away they give you good hard nips on the calves of your legs. You start to run to get away from there. After the geese there are the dogs. The first is a black-and-white ratter with a pointed nose pointed ears and tiny little eyes. He is in a hallway the door to which is always open onto the street. He is hidden in the shadows. He waits for you to go by then he comes out barking, you turn around to scare him, you kick him in the nose, he yelps as if he were crying but the minute your back is turned he quietly gives you a bite in the calves. The second dog is a ratter too, all black, smaller and faster. He doesn't bark. He lies under a cart or against the wall in the shade. He pretends not to look when you go by but he bites you in the calves just the same even if you run. When Véronique Legrand and Catherine Legrand take the road above the village besides the geese and the dogs there are some boys who lie in wait for them and attack them with nettles as they go by. You have to fight them to disarm them or else they hit Véronique Legrand and Catherine Legrand on the legs and thighs which are left bare by their short panties. They outnumber Véronique Legrand and Catherine Legrand with the result that no matter what you do you get blisters all over you don't know how. For this reason you buy yourselves pocketknives and take the road through the middle of the village to take them by surprise. They wait concealed on the other side crouching behind a wall you can sneak up from behind and attack them with your knives. Véronique Legrand and Catherine Legrand have the knives open in the palms of their hands, Véronique holds hers open in her left hand because she is left-handed, Catherine Legrand holds hers open in her right hand because she is right-handed. In this way they can easily advance side by side very close together hip to hip with the knives on the outside. It will be hard to take them by surprise. The boys turn around with their nettles the instant the girls arrive. When they see Catherine Legrand and Véronique Legrand with knives they yell something you don't understand and pounce on them throwing all the brambles in their faces on their legs on their thighs at once and running away. Mother confiscates the knives because the boys tattle to their parents. You are in front of the farm. Pascale Fromentin is in the kitchen with Aunt. You are with Pierre-Marie Fromentin and Pierre-Marie Fromentin's nanny goat. You are trying to play with the goat, you are fighting, you dodge her when she charges with her head lowered to the level of your stomach. You grab hold of her horns right where they begin, they make her forehead rough and hard, lumpy things half fleshy half bony covered with tufts of curly hair which are especially thick here. You knock her rump against the barn door by pushing her unexpectedly this makes her nervous, she charges with lowered head you barely have time to leap aside to dodge the horns. You go up the stairs. The goat can only put her front feet up the stairs. You tease her standing two steps above her taunting her with both hands so that she butts the air with her horns. You jump into the manure heap with both feet. There are corners marked out with tape. You are on the top. You walk with your feet together, you sink in to your ankles, it is dry and warm, above all you feel the straw which has been softened by rain and animal manure, it has a nice smell, Pierre-Marie Fromentin jumps higher than anyone else, you jump from the empty platform of a wooden truck, Pierre-Marie Fromentin jumps with both feet into the dung water which makes dark brown splashes on his legs and even on his thighs. You follow the cows that Uncle is about to water at the fountain. Uncle says you can take them back to the stable afterward. Catherine Legrand takes the cows back to the stable. They drink for quite a while their muzzles completely immersed then in little swallows on the surface when they aren't very thirsty any more, they graze the water lingeringly with long strings of saliva. The brim of the fountain glistens. The stone is a composite which is weathered with use. The part of the walls that is under water is green with a kind of short slimy lichen that is almost liquid. They say watercress grows in fountains but this one doesn't have any. Catherine Legrand is holding a whip with a single thong in her hand. You have to apply the thong gently and caress the buttocks of the cow who lifts her head because she has finished drinking. If you hit her hard or crack the whip instead, the cow gives a start, trots off head erect horns high and runs right by the stable. Cracking the whip doesn't work with cows. For instance if Catherine Legrand runs after a cow the cow turns around, she outruns her, and just as Catherine Legrand, flushed and winded, is about to put her hand on her to make her turn around she is off at a short, stealthy, rapid gallop. While waiting for you she browses in a ditch, she pretends to let you catch up to her, not to see that you are coming, that you are behind her and then her whole body rears and dashes forward, she gives a leap, she trots down the road not very fast so that you can follow her, so that you think you're going to catch her and don't give up right away. It is a trick because this can go on for hours. Catherine Legrand runs her hand over the cow's flanks and buttocks when she has finished drinking, Catherine Legrand presses gently and the cow turns around to go back to the stable. Catherine Legrand has put the whip under her arm as she has seen Uncle do. When the cows are all in the stable Catherine Legrand goes inside to watch them eat. The stalls are full of fresh lucerne, vetch, clover, and yellow and pink flowers which they chew to a pulp. The cow in the back has lain down. Her stomach is evenly divided between the two sides of her spine. Catherine Legrand sees that you can lie down on the cow. Catherine Legrand lies down full length on the cow, it's nice, you slip a little but you can steady yourself against the cow's back it is solid and warm the flanks on which you roll smell good of warm straw and fresh dung. Véronique Legrand wants to lie down on the cow, Pierre-Marie Fromentin wants to lie down on the cow, Pascale Fromentin wants to lie down on the cow. You take turns lying down full length on the cow who lets you do it mooing from time to time and turning her head toward you. You are on the roof of the powder mill.

The road is white with dust and sunlight you can see it between the apple trees between the strips of grass that border it on both sides. An old woman is walking bent over in dark clothing that may be black you can't tell from here. She turns off to the left into a dirt path you can't see her any more because of the trees that hide the fields. You unbolt all the sheets of lead that are on the roof all the round and overhanging collars around the screws, the washers, everything that fastens the metallic facings together. The metal is burning hot because it is directly exposed to the sun, you tear off and cut out anything that may be of lead. The piece you have in your hand seems soft already. You remember the cakes you have made. With clay. With turf. It is either one or the other this earth which cracks only on the surface when it cooks when it stays at a high temperature, and now that you have succeeded in making some evenly shaped, low but firm cakes out of it, you need something that can be molded. Vincent Parme says that lead is the easiest metal to find and the easiest to melt. On top of the cakes you melt all the lead that you collected on the roof of the powder mill. When the temperature is high enough it spreads it acts like volcanic lava you pick it up with pincers or spoons you try to make forms with it you put it in the grass to cool. You pick it up just as it is hardening among the stalks. You want to make weapons out of it. It isn't possible or else you should have thought of using an alloy to replace the lead which is brittle, your hand twists it, bends it, it has no rigidity. But you can make missiles out of it. Things like cannonballs or grenades. So you throw them at each other hot and soft or you throw them at each other cold and hard. This is how the war begins. Each has his choice of weapons. The two opposing armies come together in the plain. This is the battlefield. You are hemmed in by the river on one side by the forest on the other. So you have to fight. Vincent Parme has a small but well-trained army whose colors are red. Denise Parme has an army that yells that it wants to be the victor. You yell, you stamp on the road, you turn around to see if all is going well, you inspect each other's weapons, you criticize, you wonder if you would not do better to take a big stick like Vincent Parme's instead of a fragile sword made of a switch, a flimsy lance, anyway you stuff your pockets with grenades, you see that Véronique Legrand has a bow and the arrows that go with it, you wonder if this is not preferable even to Vincent Parme's stick. You charge with cries of God and Glory Vincent Parme yells Honor to the vanquished. You jump into the fray you fall on each other you struggle you wonder how it will all come out. There are buttocks in the air bumping heads slapping thighs. In the hurly-burly Catherine Legrand has fallen into some fresh cow dung. Everybody withdraws to his own side and you decide to start all over. After she has washed Catherine Legrand decides that she is now general of the army instead of Denise Parme. This time each general has a whistle and must blow it to move his army. Vincent Parme blows a short blast on his whistle. Catherine Legrand blows on her whistle too, but a moment later, with the result that Vincent Parme's army has already attacked Catherine Legrand's army before hers has received the order to move. You begin all over again. Facing one another are Vincent Parme Denise Parme on one side Catherine Legrand Véronique Legrand Janine Parme on the other. You fall on each other. Louis Second runs up saying that he is the general of an army. He joins Vincent Parme. You hear howls of pain. Janine Parme is bent double nursing her shin. Véronique Legrand has been hit in the eye with the stick. Denise Parme deserts and rides off on her bike. Most of the army abandons the war. Only the three generals remain on the field. Louis Second and Vincent Parme decide to take Catherine Legrand prisoner. Catherine Legrand begins to run straight ahead. Vincent Parme and Louis Second block the bridges. You are forced to go into the forest. Catherine Legrand runs through the underbrush. Low bushes, myrtles, brambles and small trees make it hard to run. Louis Second and Vincent Parme are right behind. It is cold under the trees. But Catherine Legrand feels the sweat running down each side of her face and her blouse sticks to her back. Louis Second and Vincent Parme who run fast are right behind her. They are about to catch Catherine Legrand. Catherine Legrand goes into a thicket of brambles and raspberry bushes which is higher than she is. The thorns of the brambles are the sharpest kind. It hurts, her legs immediately start to bleed. There is no retreat. The two boys hesitate before the thicket. Catherine Legrand takes the opportunity to get a head start. Vincent Parme dashes forward to try to corner Catherine Legrand right in the thicket, Louis Second walks around the thicket and waits for them to emerge. So Catherine Legrand is taken prisoner with her arms tied behind her back with two belts, she is brought back to the battlefield and neither Vincent Parme nor Louis Second yells Honor to the vanquished now. They tie her to the trunk of a tree. Louis Second has a good idea he tears off some big brambles beside the river and with all his might hits all up and down Catherine Legrand's legs and thighs which are left bare by her short panties. You decide to remove the big metal sheet that raises and lowers to let the water flow from the river to the mill. You will make a dam with it. Vincent Parme and Catherine Legrand will see how it is fastened to the ground on each side of the river. Vincent Parme and Catherine Legrand do this they crawl through the field where the grass is damp. Their bare sandaled legs sink halfway in. Every time you risk being seen you lie flat on your face and the grass wets your chest through the shirt. Vincent Parme's shirt is open so his skin is touching the damp grass. You creep forward silently. You are careful to stay next to the line of trees and bushes because the white of Vincent Parme's shirt is noticeable from every direction, you can see it from the mill, you can see it from the other side of the river, you can also see it from both bridges. You must stay close to the dark green of the hedge to advance you must be ready to fall down flat on your stomach at any moment. Catherine Legrand is less visible because of the red plaid of her blouse at night red looks like black from a distance but Vincent Parme says that you never know so whenever he flattens himself to the ground Catherine Legrand does the same and they nudge each other in the grass. You must also be very careful while examining the plank of the sluice gate— this is what you call it because you like the way it sounds but it really isn't one since there is no difference in the level of the ground and the board is there only to control the flow of water to the mill, still the whole thing looks like the sluice gate you saw on the Rhine. The board is attached to metal poles which are sunk into the bank on each side and joined together by a third pole, forming a kind of bracket. When you have unbolted it you won't be able to carry it between the two of you. You decide that several of you will come. Vincent Parme makes a deal with some boys who agree to meet at eleven o'clock at night to do it. Catherine Legrand and Vincent Parme get out of bed and get dressed in the dark. They meet at the foot of the stairs. Vincent Parme has some matches. It makes a loud noise when you scrape one on the emery paper. You go all the way to the river you don't crawl because nobody is around at this hour. You sit down in the grass on the bank. You wait. Your rear end is soaking wet. You wait. After a moment your shoulders and back are damp too. Nobody comes. You have spanners pliers pincers you have a hammer. You remove a screw that is halfway up the pole. It is difficult. It is a screw with a large head that is completely rusted it must have been there for a long time. You sit down in the grass again. Not one boy comes. You get sleepy in the grass. You tell yourself that the others are asleep in their beds. Vincent Parme gets mad, he stands up and says that those shits aren't coming, that it's just like the time you went all alone to the cemetery in the field beside the forest in the dark when Vincent Parme and Catherine Legrand took turns going there alone and not one of the others went and afterward the shits said it was because of the will-o'-the-wisps. Catherine Legrand says that you explained to them that it is a chemical phenomenon but this didn't keep them from continuing to say No, they are dead people. So after a while you go back to bed. You are walking through the grass in the meadows that line the forest. You see the light turning the trunks of the fir trees blue and the branches higher up making green webs on a blue background. You see how the light is of another color to the side, the color of mica but more intense almost orange. The sunlight falling between the trunks makes bars that look solid. The trees form cylinders perpendicular to the ground and parallel to each other long verticals that rise side by side in a pattern that is crossed at regular intervals by the oblique lines, cylinders or cones of light that form masses equal to the trunks. You walk silently because of the hares. You want to see them sleeping in the grass they make their holes here because it is cooler than the under-growth. If you flush one by the time you come to his hole he has already run away with his ears spread flopping against his back so that you never see them sleeping no matter how quietly you come up to them. Suddenly Vincent Parme almost stops and holds out his arm so Catherine Legrand will stop too. There is a snake sleeping in the sun in the grass. It is short and loosely coiled. Vincent Parme goes up and grabs it behind the head with his thumb and index finger. The snake starts to wriggle but it has already lost contact with the ground it is now in the hands of Catherine Legrand who watches the tongue flick in and out then Catherine Legrand asks Vincent Parme if he is giving it to her and Vincent Parme laughs and says, It was for you that I caught it. Catherine Legrand almost drops the snake which tries to slip between her fingers because she doesn't know how to hold it. Then she slips it into the sleeve of her blouse wraps it around the wrist of her left hand and arranges it so that it is warm and so that the triangular head rests in her palm. The snake stops moving, when he tries to get away Catherine Legrand folds her fingers against her palm to keep him from doing it. Vincent Parme spits on the ground and says that they won't find anything to give him to eat. You start to look for ants. Vincent Parme says red ants are good for snakes you look for the little mounds they make in the grass that way you will find eggs too. You don't find red ants you only find black ants but the snake doesn't want them you put them near him you try to put them on his tongue which he keeps flicking in and out he doesn't swallow them. Vincent Parme says he is only a baby snake he doesn't eat because he is afraid. Catherine Legrand says it is because he doesn't like ants. So you decide that he will eat tadpoles. Vincent Parme says he knows where you can find some. To do this you have to walk through the village at the longest part where it runs along the national highway. You pass the town hall and the school. On the wall of the school on one side of the big door it says Girls' School and on the other side Boys' School. In front of the town hall and the school is the square with the monument to the dead, the church is on the other side. From a distance you can see the pink gravel under the trees with the big bright leaves and when you walk parallel to the town hall and the school if you look to the right you can see the red brick of the building through the leaves of the sycamores and just below the main branches. There is green paint on the benches. If you put some women Indian file both sideways and frontways at the same time standing and sitting it would look like Gauguin's marketplace. The tarred national highway is melting because it is unprotected from the sun. You are perspiring. Vincent Parme's face is red. Catherine Legrand's face is purple. The shops are empty and dark, you don't hear the click of the long strings of wooden beads that screen the sun in front of the doors. You drag your feet. You stop by the sewers. You are looking for an empty tin can to put the tadpoles in. There isn't one to be found in the village. And yet you are sure you remember playing Kick the Can on the national highway. At last you find one at the edge of the village beyond the billboard, half buried in the dirt of the embankment, you must have overlooked it because of its color. You are at the unused fountain. There isn't a breath of air. The spring that fed it doesn't flow any more, the water in the basin is from the last rains. The side walls are green with stagnant water. Here are tadpoles in the first phase of development they have big vibratile tails with which they move. They look like spermatozoa. Others already resemble small frogs and swim away as fast as they can when you cast a shadow over the water. You pick the more mature ones because they're fatter. You move your hand in the thick lukewarm water. Now you can't see anything any more because the mud rises to the surface spreads everywhere remains in suspension in the water. You take out your hands. You wait for the water to clear again. You take a stick to search the mud without making it rise, this way you chase the tadpoles from the solid layer in which they are hiding. When you put the snake in the washbowl with the first tadpole nothing happens it's no use putting the snake's mouth on the tadpole he acts as if he were blind. But he is all excited though. The tadpole is all excited too he tries to crawl up the smooth side of the washbowl, he falls back, he begins again, suddenly the snake notices the smell, he stiffens to locate it, he slithers along making rings around the little animal with his body, the last, very narrow ring formed by the snake's head and neck catches the tadpole. The snake opens his mouth very wide and swallows the tadpole you can see his hind legs moving. The snake struggles with the motion in his mouth, he swallows, you can see that the tadpole is wedged in his gullet, that he is still moving, that he is moving through the snake's body making a lump in it. The snake seems sleepy. This doesn't keep him from stiffening again when you give him a new tadpole. The snake swallows ten tadpoles one after the other. It is his olfactory sense that enables him to catch them after much slithering and groping, you can see his tongue crawling against the earthenware of the washbowl. You are all out of tadpoles. You go to see Aunt. Catherine Legrand has the snake rolled around her wrist. She sits down at the table. Catherine Legrand can't help raising the sleeve of her blouse to show the snake. Everybody begins screaming around the table. Chairs are pushed back. Catherine Legrand says that the snake isn't bad she puts him around her neck to show that he isn't bad but this does not prevent her from being put out of the house. Catherine Legrand isn't allowed to keep the snake inside the house. He is in the yard in a shoebox with holes punched in it. Catherine Legrand can't sleep because she is afraid someone will come and take the snake so she gets up and goes barefoot to look for him outdoors. She feels dried dog feces crumbling beneath her feet. Catherine Legrand wipes her feet on the blanket before slipping between the sheets. After she has lain down she feels in the dark for the shoebox. Then Catherine Legrand removes the cover of the box, feels inside with the tips of her fingers until she touches the coiled body of the snake and unrolls him, she feels her way to the head so she can take him into bed with her. Catherine Legrand sleeps with the snake rolled around her arm which she has stretched out across the bed so she won't crush him beneath her in her sleep. You have to stay at the table for a long time it's tiring you rock your chair back and forth. Vincent Parme Denise Parme Janine Parme Véronique Legrand Catherine Legrand are there. Véronique Legrand is making little men out of bread. She spits on it she kneads it to make it homogenous. Véronique Legrand makes a first group of balls for the heads, she puts them in a row at the edge of the table. You watch her do it as you rock back and forth on your chair. Véronique Legrand makes a second group of fatter balls and these she forms into ovals, they are the bodies. Véronique Legrand puts each body and head together. She spits on both parts to glue them together. She sticks matches into them for arms and legs. Unfortunately the little men won't stand up. Janine Parme whips out her hand and takes one of Véronique Legrand's little men puts it on the edge of her plate and walks it all around. Véronique Legrand gets mad and tries to take back her little man saying, Why don't you make your own give me back my little man. Meanwhile the little man that Janine Parme is holding in her hands and defending by lying half over the plate is marching into the mashed potato, he leaves prints in it like the ones birds make in the sand. Finally Janine Parme sticks him into the thickest part of the mashed potato where he goes in up to his waist, where he stands up. Suddenly Véronique Legrand who has been watching pounces on Janine Parme's plate she leans forward and almost recovers the little man. Janine Parme has him in her closed hands, she defends him by hitting with her elbows. This doesn't prevent the little man from getting crushed in Janine Parme's palms when Véronique Legrand tries to pry open her fingers. Denise Parme also takes the little breadcrumb men. Véronique Legrand defends them and screams but all her little men have now been taken away from her. And you throw Véronique Legrand's little men in one another's faces and Véronique Legrand also begins to throw all the little men that she picks up the minute they fall in the faces of Vincent Parme Denise Parme Janine Parme Catherine Legrand. Suddenly Vincent Parme picks up his plate and hurls all the mashed potato into Denise Parme's face you can see it steaming on her. You look at Denise Parme and laugh she yells rubs her eyes full of mashed potato gets some of it in her hair grabs her own plate and throws the warm mashed potato back at Vincent Parme who ducks just in time so that there is a big glob of mashed potato steaming and dripping down the wall in back of him. The fathers and mothers get mad through the open door you see them at the other table pushing back their chairs standing up yelling by the table where everybody is now covered with mashed potato. So you run off to the bathroom to wash. You push each other in front of the washbowl. You hit each other with your fists on the back and face. Catherine Legrand chases Vincent Parme with the tube of toothpaste in her hand. You see him fall onto his bed. Catherine Legrand jumps on top of him and mounts his stomach squeezing the tube of toothpaste onto his cheeks, into his ears, into his neck, onto his back, along the nape of his neck where you can feel the skin behind the cloth of the shirt. Vincent Parme rolls on the bedsheets to wipe himself off. Catherine Legrand is still on top of him she doesn't let him go she empties the tube completely she runs away. You are going to look for apples in the wheat fields. You walk between the ripe, pale-yellow ears. You walk bent over among the stalks so that your head won't show above the level of the wheat. You hear people harvesting in the next field. From time to time you lift your head and see the whole wheat field and the apple tree you want to reach and the red apples which are on top. You see that some men and women are mowing and it makes a shiny cut at the base of the stalks and a whole row of wheat falls down silently like water. You stop to rest. You sit on the ground. You are surrounded by stalks of wheat the ears are enormous against the blue of the sky seen from below like this. The poppies are weighing down their soft stalks some of which are even twisted. The cornflowers have stiffer stalks. When you get up you see white scarves that look like handkerchiefs and straw hats on the heads in the other field. Then you keep on crawling to the tree the wheat is thinner around it, leaving a space where grass has grown. You creep into the tree without making any noise being careful that none of the harvesters sees you. When you are back on the ground you divide the apples. You are sitting at the foot of the tree. You start to eat one without talking. In the curve of the fruit you see the shape of your teeth, the scallop of skin certain parts of which have not been cut neatly and still stick half-chewed to the flesh of the apple. You put the apples that are left into your shirt holding them against your chest. You leave, crawling through the stalks of wheat. Suddenly you look up and see a man's cap coming toward you. So you start to run openly through the field. You throw away apples every few steps so you can run faster because now you have too many, they are in your hand for a moment, a red more orange than the poppies, they roll at the base of the wheat and disappear. You run for a long time so you will outstrip the man then you get down to the level of the wheat you start to walk on all fours between the stalks trying not to make the wheat ripple so they won't spot you from a distance because sometimes when a mouse runs away it looks as if a knife were running the whole length of a wheat field. After a moment you stop and sit down on the ground. You don't talk. You listen to the sounds. You hear the jerky flights of insects very close. When these have finished you hear silence then a continuous drone which seems to come from a distance. You realize that this is the sound made by all the insects who are flying at that moment, that it is a very loud noise completely separate from the sound of the people who are in the fields. You realize from this drone that there is a different world to which you can't possibly belong. You rub your ears because the drone gets more and more insistent more and more continuous you begin to hear it as a single and unbearable shrillness, you end up wondering whether it doesn't come from yourself, you even plug your ears, but when you take your fingers away it is still there. Every once in a while a big fly or a honey bee or a hornet comes close, then there is a mechanical sound an individual hum with a precise origin then it turns into the other sound, the great background sound, and is drowned out. Sometimes you think you hear footsteps approaching, you huddle against the ground, you feel your heart beating against your knees which you hold tight against your chest. A shrew mouse or a rat goes by and stops. You wait in the middle of the wheat for the sun to go down. Then the people leave the fields. They are full of colors at this hour because the light is not harsh. Along the forest there are large ocher shadows on the wheat, beneath the trees there are big dark spots that look like ink blots, there are ultramarines that fall on the strips of forest that you see at the bottom of the sky, beyond you can't see anything because it's the horizon, but anyway you can see very well that the earth is round because the line that divides the transparent blue of the sky from the ultramarine of the forest makes a dark and unmistakable curve, when you turn around you see something like a great ring as round as any circle and over your head you see the sky in the shape of an empty orange that you have cut in two to make a hemisphere. You wipe off the dirt that you have on your seat from sitting down. You get back on the road. You hear the bell of some village. The insect drone has died down you can hardly hear it any more even if you listen closely. A kind of coolness falls onto the wheat and the grass of the embankment where you are. You are walking in the forest. You hear an ax striking a tree somewhere. The dog is waiting for you sitting in the middle of the road, tongue lolling, you can see his saliva running out of his mouth. Even when you can't see him because of the winding of the road you can hear him panting. He stops every once in a while to run his tongue over the saliva that covers his coat. It is very hot. Because they are transparent you can see the veins of the leaves that are in the sun clearly, all together they make a green and translucent mass like the water in an aquarium. When you walk in the clearings and when the sun is not blocked by a screen it hits you smack on the face and arms and thighs, you have pins and needles on your scalp because of the rays which find their way through your hair to the skin. You have some milk cans. You drop them on the stones of the road to hear the noise they make. You pick them up. You throw them against the trees to make a different sound. After a while they are all dented. So you roll them along the road with your feet. The dog begins to squeal because he got kicked on the nose. They say that dogs have sensitive noses. Vincent Parme was kicking the can away, aiming at the clump of bushes, but the dog was right behind it. You comfort him. You pat him. He licks your hands your faces and your knees. You come to the abandoned quarry. It is covered with brambles. Through them you can see a pale yellow, you don't know whether it is rock salt or weathered limestone. Even the rails are overgrown with blackberry and raspberry bushes. You can see that they are very rusty you can get rust powder by scraping them with a stout stick. Afterward you wipe your hands on your bloomers on your thighs on your knees which makes you orange all over. You find an overturned tip truck in the bushes, the bin is dented and has holes in it in places and is half torn off the wheels. Vincent Parme tries to put the truck right side up yelling, Help me, for God's sake. You help him. You can't do it because the whole thing is stuck in the ground. You groan. You perspire. Vincent Parme says, When I say three everybody push, one two three. Suddenly the truck comes loose and rights itself. Vincent Parme is saying one two three. At three you give such a shove that the truck falls over the other way and you fall on top of it every which way. Anyway now you can move it you even manage to get it back onto a section of rail. Then you climb into it and take turns pushing each other. The wheels are twisted and the rails are twisted so they don't really fit together the cart is forever falling over so that whoever is in it must jump out quick or get caught under the bin. The dog runs after the truck jumping and barking and trying to catch Véronique Legrand Denise Parme Janine Parme Vincent Parme Catherine Legrand. After a moment he gets tired, he goes and lies down in the shade under some low bushes. His tongue is still hanging out of his mouth. When he rests his muzzle on his front paws which are stretched out in front of him he puts his tongue in because he is afraid of getting it on the ground. He stays like that with his eyes half closed but he has to lift his head every once in a while so he can let his tongue hang down and start panting again. You get bored with the truck. You push it into a bramble patch where it loses balance and falls slowly over into the tangled branches. You start picking raspberries and blackberries. You eat as many as you can. Denise Parme takes some blackberries in each hand and begins to smear Janine Parme's cheeks with them, she has them everywhere on her chin even in her hair, then you attack each other with blackberries you try to smear each other, you put them on each other's

123

shirts and arms when you can't reach the faces. In the end you are really purple especially your cheeks you can just see the eyes all white somewhere above. You have eaten so many blackberries and raspberries that you feel like throwing up. Then you start filling the cans, some with blackberries, others with raspberries. Suddenly Véronique Legrand upsets the can of blackberries which is between her and Catherine Legrand and the berries roll out. Catherine Legrand jumps up yelling that all their work is for nothing and scattering every which way the blackberries that remained in the can and throwing the can as far as she can into the quarry where you hear it ring against a stone. Vincent Parme Janine Parme Denise Parme burst out laughing one after the other they look at each other and they look at Catherine Legrand and they laugh harder and harder, then Véronique Legrand starts to laugh too, Catherine Legrand who is now very red tries to stare them down but they don't stop laughing and they even jump up and down until Vincent Parme starts to empty his own can around him until Denise Parme and Janine Parme empty their cans around them, until Denise Parme Vincent Parme Janine Parme start to dance around Catherine Legrand swinging the empty cans in their hands until they throw them as far as they can into the quarry where you hear them fall some against stumps others against stones until there are no more blackberries no more raspberries no more cans. You pass the caretaker's house. No one is living there because it isn't the sea-son when the grapes are ripe yet. On the back of the house there are metal brackets placed one over the other to form a ladder by which you can get to the roof. When you are up there you are on a terrace that covers the whole house. You can see the parallel rows of grapevines running down the hills. You can see hills covered with forests that are almost black, you can see grassy hills that look blue, you can see the plain below with the villages which look as if they were very close together. When you are on the terrace you feel as if you were in Babylon with its tiered terraces descending like steps to the Euphrates, with its flowering trees and hanging gardens. You feel like lying on your stomach on the cement and staying there and looking at the grass, the grapevines, the forests, looking at the birds, the hills, you feel like turning over onto your back and watching the clouds go by, you feel like staying there to watch the sky darken and all the stars come out. Catherine Legrand says that you will come that night and sleep on the terrace of the caretaker's house that you could learn to recognize the stars and call them by their names. You are walking on the road that goes along the forest on one side while the other overlooks the vineyards. You can't see anything but the vineyards even though you are on the crest of the hill. You try to pick out Uncle's vineyard where Catherine Legrand says you can eat as many grapes as you like. You walk halfway down to a road that runs across the hill perpendicular to the rows of vines. You march.

You say as you go by, It's not that one, it's not that one. Suddenly you say, It's that one, and you stop because of a big white stone stuck in the ground which Catherine Legrand recognizes. You start off again because Catherine Legrand says she isn't really sure, that the white stone at the end of Uncle's field might be bigger or smaller, or there might be two of them like in this field you are now passing. You stop again in front of a single white stone, this one isn't round, it looks more like a boundary stone. Catherine Legrand is undecided she does and does not recognize Uncle's field. You walk some more you come to some piles of bricks, you come to some stakes driven into the ground, you even come to some dwarf apricot trees, all this below the fields at the end of the road, you even come to a plot of white stones, of crushed blocks. Catherine Legrand says that you must have passed Uncle's field so you turn back. You look and stop in front of each field. Suddenly Catherine Legrand says, Here it is I'm positive, so you pounce on the grapes you tear off big half-black grapes, you begin to suck the juice because you're thirsty, then you notice that there are places where the grapes are riper, so you throw everything you have into the next vineyard, you eat right from the bunch without picking the grapes, you sit on the ground at the foot of the vine and eat right from the branch, pulling the bunch with your teeth, crushing the grapes with your lips and teeth they roll away from you because you aren't using your hands so that you look like Romulus and Remus sucking the she-wolf. After a moment Catherine Legrand says you aren't in the right field so you hurry between the vine props stooping under the wires that bind them together. You find yourself in a field which Catherine Legrand recognizes as Uncle's. You begin eating grapes again all green and all blue ones. You pull off the grapes in handfuls, for fun you squeeze the bunches in your hands keeping your fingers closed. You realize that you still aren't in the right field. You move to the next field, then to the next and so on Catherine Legrand recognizes them all one after the other as Uncle's, so you make a stop in each one, you come and go along the vines, you cross the whole hill now running bent over under the branches under the tendrils under the layers which you can see hanging from the wires and which make straight rows from the top of the hill down to the last road the one that runs around the hill in the plain. Suddenly Janine Parme stops clutching her stomach with both hands and yelling for you to wait for her. You see her crouching behind a vine stock. Denise Parme Vincent Parme Véronique Legrand Catherine Legrand take turns crouching behind vine stocks, everybody has the runs now, you wipe yourself with those leaves that people put on the fronts of statues. Janine Parme is the first to finish. You walk behind her fixing your clothes. Your intestines are full of sulfate and the acidity of unripe grapes it tears like cigarette paper when you touch it, it feels like ground glass in your stomach. You are in a hurry to get home.

You run down the hill, stopping from time to time behind the vines, trying to hold it as long as possible but when one person begins to shit the others can't help doing the same, you hurry, you are pursued by a stench which is gaining ground it gets there before you do unless you have it on you by now that smell of grapes decomposing or fermenting. The hay is harvested. The barns are open. All the dry grass is piled in the upper lofts where it has been pitched with forks where it is now packed so tightly that the lofts look emptier than before. The barrows that were cluttering the middle part of the barn have been pushed back because now there is no room for them in this place since the leftover hay is piled there in stacks and leaning against the partitions all around. There is a smell of dried flowers and grasses. If you stand still with your head lolling you get drunk because the smell is everywhere, you can feel it in your nostrils in your ears you can feel it moving inside your head, but above all it is in your skin all over your body, the pores are open, they start to secrete the smells of grass of dandelions of cornflowers of poppies of oats and of vetch and you couldn't say which grass or flower smells the strongest, you go crazy and begin to run in the upper haylofts, you jump from one to the other over the open hatches. The breeze that comes into the barn stirs the stalks that stick out of the piles of hay, sometimes you get whiffs of a stronger smell. Pascale Fromentin Pierre-Marie Fromentin Véronique Legrand Catherine Legrand jump on the piles of hay, you try to bump your head against the crossbeams. Sometimes you lose your balance then you fall you wallow in the clover in the grains in the long daisies you burrow your face into them you sniff you chew pieces of grass you scratch your cheeks. Pierre-Marie Fromentin trips Véronique Legrand and just as she falls down Pierre-Marie Fromentin throws an armful of hay as big as she is which he was holding ready for that purpose on top of her. You hear smothered laughter and shrieking. Véronique Legrand struggles as hard as she can to come to the surface. You see the hay undulating in the place where she is, arch its back stir in masses while Pierre-Marie Fromentin pushes down on it to keep her under. Finally Véronique Legrand succeeds in kicking Pierre-Marie Fromentin in the face he lets go and yells because he got a good kick in the nose. You see Véronique Legrand come out from under the hay red-faced and winded you can't tell where the hay leaves off and her hair begins she even has stalks coming right out of her ears. You walk along the edge of the hayloft crossing the partition that divides the barn from the stable, from the high loft where you are you look at the lower middle part of the barn where the carts are kept but where right now there is a big pile of hay which forms a kind of haystack. Pascale Fromentin jumps from the hayloft where you are to the haystack down below, you watch her sink in to her waist, she looks very small seen from above, Pierre-Marie Fromentin jumps and of course Véronique Legrand and Catherine Legrand jump after him. You land softly you sink into all that smell, you are completely drunk, you dash to the ladder to be the first one up to be the first one to jump. You jump over and over. You jostle each other to get to the ladder. You push the person in front of you who doesn't go up the rungs fast enough. You hear the animals stirring in the stable because of the smell of the hay. Your skin is so scratched up by the grass that even under your clothes it feels flayed bare and salted, so that you have a cutaneous pain which is the same everywhere except between your legs where it's even worse, it stings like a cut. Suddenly you see Pascale Fromentin swerve in her fall for some reason, you see her land on the edge of the haystack, you see her hand get impaled on one of the teeth of the harrow. The harrow is leaning against the wall and gleaming dully half hidden by the grass that you stirred up by jumping. Pascale Fromentin frees her hand, you can't hear her say anything but you see the wound which is immediately covered with blood the minute she separates her hand from the steel, you see that Pascale Fromentin is dead white so you gather around her. It is raining. You are in the hut that you made for yourselves in the forest. Véronique Legrand and Janine Parme are baking apples in the clay oven. They put them in the oven without noticing that someone has melted lead there, on the twisted strips of zinc, along the curves and on the flat part there are drops of solidified lead which remain solid because the oven is not at their melting point. It looks like frozen mercury. Véronique Legrand and Janine Parme are looking after the cooking of the apples, poking them and turning them over with sticks. When one of the apples is done Véronique Legrand or Janine Parme pulls it out by impaling it with one of the sticks. It has turned from light green to brown it oozes a little the skin is crackled, the whole surface of the apple is soft and limp, but the center isn't cooked. Véronique Legrand pulls out an apple. It is shriveled around the stick, you can see lead sticking to the skin the lead shines from the juice that runs out of the apple when it cooks. Véronique Legrand puts it on a pile of sand which has been put in the hut to keep supplies on. Those that are cooked and cooled and ready to eat are all sandy. So you put the new ones which are boiling hot on a pile of ash, elm and beech leaves. Vincent Parme is reading. Catherine Legrand is reading. You hear the rain hitting the leaves of the roof of the hut. Vincent Parme bursts out laughing and puts his picture book in front of Catherine Legrand on top of the reader she is reading. Catherine Legrand sees that Vincent Parme is laughing because Captain Haddock was transformed into a little bird cheep cheep cheep while pursuing his bottle of whiskey. Catherine Legrand tries to read what happens next but Vincent Parme snatches back the book for himself alone and hides it with his arms so you can't read along with him.

So Catherine Legrand goes back to turning the pages of the reader stopping at *Braided pearls bound to her temples fell to the corners of her parted lips, which were pink as a pomegranate. On her bosom there lay a variety of luminous gems that rivaled the scales of the muraena.* The scene is Carthage. You have learned a rule of Latin grammar and in the example Carthage is discussed in these terms, *Ceterum, censeo Carthaginem esse delendam,* either Cato's phrase or the rule of the gerund or the predicate adjective. In the reader there are only abridged texts, bits selected you wonder by whom, at least you'd like to know what came before and after, but you have the feeling you never will. Anyway ten lines read like that in a book aren't interesting. For this reason Catherine Legrand prefers to repeat one of the passages over and over until it means something to her and this way sometimes she finds one she really likes. When you are allowed to read whole books you will find the sentences you have memorized in them: *Braided pearls bound to her temples fell to the corners of her parted lips, which were pink as a pomegranate. On her bosom there lay a variety of luminous gems that rivaled the scales of the muraena.* Catherine Legrand asks Vincent Parme what a muraena is. Vincent Parme says, Leave me alone. He has almost finished his picture book and you realize you can't make him look up. Catherine Legrand snatches away the book that he has on his knees saying, I'll give it back to you if you tell me what a muraena is.

Vincent Parme jumps up and down in front of Catherine Legrand waving his arms in all directions over her head and to the sides trying to grab the book which she is holding behind her back and saying It must be a fish if it has scales. Catherine Legrand gives him back the book saying How big and Vincent Parme shrugs his shoulders and goes and sits down in his corner. Véronique Legrand is making a little man out of a stick. The knife is now in her right hand now in her left hand depending on which is more convenient to carve the stick at the angle she chooses. She is the first to yell that it's raining in the hut. In fact the leaves of the roof, which were taken from elms, beeches, ashes and even from birches and were all shriveled and dry, are finally letting the water in. Now that they are wet they are even smaller and you can see the sky through the roof of the hut the raindrops are falling like needles right into your eyes which would be stabbed if you didn't close them in time but it's only water. So you put all your property, the books the apples the knives the playing cards in the part of the hut which still keeps out the rain. You go into the forest to cut branches. You must put a new layer of foliage on the roof of the hut to keep out the water. You walk through the dense, damp underbrush. Since the terrain slopes and you are going uphill you help yourself up by holding onto the shrubs, suckers, and all the branches growing out of the ground which do not have prickers. All the water on them gets on your clothes so that your arms, your shirts, your legs and your thighs are all soaking wet. You can hear water falling everywhere on the leaves on the trunks on the roads, the sound of running water is in your ears, it is a summer of springs, but it is raining the forest is gray, brown, black in places. You have two axes. You decide to cut fir branches because the needles don't change size even when they are dry, this is why they make the best roofs. You cut the young fir shoots, you cut the lower branches when there are any. You try to get big branches so you can spread them all the way across the roof without adding anything else. When you are done you make piles you go back down each person drags his pile behind him, the needles stick together, the branches get tangled, this keeps the piles from staying apart. You hear the steady sound of the branches scraping along the leaf floor of the forest. Janine Parme tries to detach herself from a bramble and catches her whole pile of branches in the bramble bush. You have to put down all the piles and help her untangle hers from the branches of shrubs that hang down verti-cally and catch those being dragged horizontally with their thorns or twigs. You are at Uncle's burial. You wait by the door until everybody is ready. You look at the hens on the manure heap and on the steps of the house. You hear the cows moving in the stable. The window of the room where the coffin is is open and a smell comes out of it. Catherine Legrand and Véronique Legrand hear the women who are standing nearby whisper that it is the body. There are a lot of people. Men in the suits they wear to go to mass on Sunday. Women in black dresses and round hats, these are also their Sunday clothes. Everyone talks in a low voice. The house is on the road to church, so they stopped off on the way from church. Now they must take out the coffin for the second time. Four men carry it down the stairs giving each other instructions so they won't drop it. Behind them Aunt walks down the steps in a big veil that comes in front of her face. Pascale Fromentin and Pierre-Marie Fromentin are with her. The men lay the coffin on the litter which is at the foot of the stairs. Now it is the litter that they carry, two are in front, two are in back, each supports an arm on his shoulder. A black cloth with tassels is placed over the coffin. You see the white crosses which are laid on each side against the coffin. The priest has a surplice on over his black robe, he has a black stole on. The priest begins to walk behind the coffin. He holds an open mass book in front of him. Beside him the choirboy carries the pail of holy water and the aspergillum. Aunt, Pascale Fromentin, and Pierre-Marie Fromentin begin to walk behind too, everyone gets in line, first members of the family, then people. You pass the last houses of the village. You walk right through the fields on a dirt road bleached by the sun it hurts your eyes to look at it. In the distance almost in the forest you see the chapel by the cemetery, you see the walls that enclose it. The men carrying the coffin advance slowly. You are behind them, on each side of the road are clipped fields here and there there are still big tracks of dried grass which the rakes haven't caught. There are fields in which there is nothing left but the stubble of wheat, oats and barley. Nobody says anything. It is hot. The stream that flows beside the road doesn't make its usual gushing sound now and then you can just hear a splash. On the banks the last flowers are fading. The priest recites the prayers in Latin and you say the responses. There are long silences. Then you hear the sobs of Aunt, of Pascale Fromentin, of Pierre-Marie Fromentin, of other people you don't know. The priest begins a new prayer, you answer him, Amen, *requiescat in pace*, et cetera. You watch the coffin wobble from left to right over the heads of the pallbearers. You hear the sound the shoes make dragging along the ground, the crowd is trampling like a herd. When you turn around you see that the whole burial procession is only a tiny black spot in the middle of the fields. You walk. Every once in a while you stop so the pallbearers can change shoulders. It is hot. You are perspiring. Black must hold in the heat. Sometimes you trip on a stone because you're walking so slowly and because it's hard to lift your feet in this heat. Swallows fly low, uttering little cries when they meet or pass each other. When you reach the cemetery you see that the gravedigger is still in the hole throwing dirt behind him. The litter is laid down. The coffin is lowered with ropes.

The priest says some prayers taking the aspergillum from the hands of the choirboy, sprinkling the grave with holy water, handing the aspergillum to Aunt. Someone, a man, plays a farewell to the dead man on a trumpet, it makes a sound that splits your ears and won't go away. Then Aunt falls to her knees on the earth of the grave you hear the cries she makes as the first shovelful of dirt is thrown onto the wood of the coffin. You hear the sobs of Pierre-Marie Fromentin who has fallen to his knees. Pascale Fromentin is very small and all hunched up between them. You hear the sobs of the women in front and in back.

Au grant palais de la sale pavée estait *Guibors s'ot l'aubert endousée le haime ou cief et au costé l'espée ainc n'i ot dame ne fust le jor armée.* The pages of the open notebook are cross-ruled. Vertical and longitudinal lines are printed inside squares whose sides are emphasized by thicker lines this is how you can tell they are squares. Their sides must be one centimeter. Almost the size of a written letter. You put the letters inside the squares. There are some letters that don't fit for example the b's the l's the t's and above all the p's which you can't possibly keep inside the squares. Nicole Marre is next to Catherine Legrand. She is drawing a gargoyle in the margin of her notebook to mark the beginning of the chapter on Aliscans. Catherine Legrand is trying to draw Guibourc with coat of mail helmet and sword and wondering whether she ought to make her dress hang down below the coat of mail to show that she is a lady. Catherine Legrand leaves a blank space for the legs and feet or for the dress which might have a train in back. Catherine Legrand draws every link of the coat of mail they look like scales, Guibourc is a fish without a tail one eye is bigger than the other under the helmet so Catherine Legrand erases Guibourc and draws the battlements of the Tower of Orange. When you stand up in back you can see the cypress trees on the plain. Mother of the Infant Jesus asks Marielle Balland to summarize the passage you have just read and for which you wrote the words you didn't understand in your notebooks followed by a colon and their origin and meaning. Marielle Balland tells how Guibourc and the women of Orange defended the town against the Saracens, *Lassus fu grans et ruste la mellée les dames ont mainte piere jetée maint Sarrasin ont la teste quassée ki gisent mort sovin geule baée.* Orange was not taken, there it is in broad daylight and Guibourc is perspiring heavily under the coat of mail and pushing up the helmet that covers her eyes. Mother of the Infant Jesus says that there once was a land in the south, she says that the king of

France came on horseback with a mighty army to destroy this land, she says that he called this a crusade, she says that since this time there has never been a civilization that can compare with that of this land. You write in your notebook, Albigensian Crusade. In the first row to the right of Nicole Marre and Catherine Legrand are Marielle Balland and Sophie Rieux, to their right Laurence Bouniol and Valerie Borge. You have black smocks on. Marielle Balland has on a leather belt with links at the sides. She has hung a pocket knife from one of the links. *Mes filles, soutenez votre reine éperdue.* It is Esther whose knees tremble now shrouded in veils. Mother of the Infant Jesus is giving the lesson in sacred history and telling the story of Esther. You write in your notebook, Bible, Book of Esther. When you stoop down to pick up your ruler or eraser you see Marielle Balland's knees Sophie Rieux's knees, Laurence Bouniol's knees, Valerie Borge's knees. Valerie Borge is leaning her head on her left arm. Mother of the Infant Jesus remarks on this and asks whether Valerie Borge would like *her* elbow as well. The trees have lost some of their leaves. There are still quite a few left but their color has faded especially those on the chestnut trees which are shriveled and brown. You walk in the playground in groups. The boarders talk among themselves and refuse to play ball. The day pupils decide to play volley ball in the yard with the statue where the net is set up. Nicole Marre runs off to get the ball. She passes Laurence Bouniol yelling, *Rois Desramés a sa barbe jurée*, and Laurence Bouniol replies as she goes by, *Ke Guibors ert à cevaus traïnée* and Julienne Pont and Marielle Balland who are also running by continue with *Et en la mer noïe et esfondrée.* At noon you shake hands saying, *Rois Desramés a sa barbe jurée ke Guibors ert à cevaux traïnée et en la mer noïe et esfondrée.* You burst out laughing when you come to *Mais je quit bien sa barbe ert parjurée.* It is time to go home for lunch. You do it again at one twenty-five, before the bell rings. You shake hands and say, *Rois Desramés a sa barbe jurée,* et cetera, you know it by heart now. Noémie Mazat is wearing a gray blouse that is ripped in back. She has on hobnailed boots. When you sing, Pretty lad when you dance, tap your heels and make them ring, you think of her. Anne-Marie Brunet is a boarder, Sophie Rieux Anne Gerlier Denise Causse Marie Démone Valerie Borge are boarders. They stop beside the wall between the two yards and keep on talking. Meanwhile Anne Gerlier has sat down and put a wool cardigan around her shoulders. You are in the infirmary. Mother of Saint Francis of Assisi has left. Through the open window you can see the trees and the high wall that separates the garden of the school from that of the convent. When you climb up on the wall to look into the garden of the convent you don't see the nuns with black veils in front of their faces you see neat paths and grass plots bordered with trimmed box, dwarf carnations, poet's despair and forget-menots marked out with string. In the shade between the rows of flowers small round acacia leaves are sticking to the ground. Denise Causse is lying in bed in the infirmary. You see that her cheeks are red. Mother of Saint Francis of Assisi has forbidden Catherine Legrand to speak to her because it would tire her. Mother of Saint Francis of Assisi has prepared Catherine Legrand's inhalation. Catherine Legrand leans over the steaming bowl but not too far because it is hot. Mother of Saint Francis of Assisi puts her black wool shawl over Catherine Legrand's head and the bowl so that the steam will stay localized around Catherine Legrand's nose. The shawl has a familiar smell. All of a sudden it hurts your chest or somewhere else your stomach or between your legs. Catherine Legrand can't stand the pain she sticks her head out of the black wool shawl and makes faces at Denise Causse. Denise Causse has raised herself onto one elbow and asks Catherine Legrand in a whisper to stay with her not to go away to tell Mother of Saint Francis of Assisi that she feels very sick now and wants to go to bed. But Catherine Legrand doesn't want to go to bed with that smell all over the room the smell of the cooled infusion and the smell of ether still lingering in the air. Catherine Legrand throws the shawl all the way off and waits for the bowl of inhalation to cool and for Mother of Saint Francis of Assisi to return to the infirmary. You are playing war in Saint Germain des Champs. You run up the hill. You count off under the acacias.

You wait there a moment because Max Gibrol has not arrived. The grocery store is right next to the other side of the terrace bordered with acacia trees. The flowers have a smell that goes to your head. You feel like kicking their trunks. Madame Henri comes out of the grocery store with the idiot girl who giggles and shakes her head from side to side and kicks in the shins a lady who is coming in just as they are leaving. Madame Henri shakes the idiot girl as hard as she can so she will behave. The girl lolls her head and slobbers. Christiane Gibrol shows Catherine Legrand a lady walking across the terrace with a baby in her stomach. Christiane Gibrol begins to yell, Come on Max, with all her might holding her hands in front of her mouth to make a loudspeaker. Jacques Lamasse runs down the hill and back up and says that Max Gibrol is busy rollerskating and doesn't want to come. You divide into three sides. You go and hide behind a group of houses in some yards behind the open main gate. You lie in ambush for each other. At your feet or beside you if you are squatting you have the bullets or grenades that you have made from the red claylike dirt of Saint Germain des Champs. You have one ready at the end of a stick you put as many as you can in your pockets the rest are on the ground. When you see an enemy go by you throw a grenade pow! right in his face the clay breaks and you fit another to the end of the stick before the enemy has time to open his eyes. As a rule it is always the side Max

Gibrol is on that wins and this isn't surprising because everyone wants to be on the same side he is therefore there is always one side that is three times as big as the other or others and that wins. Today you can't tell who will win. You fight blindly. Christiane Gibrol reinforces the grenades with pebbles. You stick them in when the enemy gets one in the face it hurts even more. The prisoners are tied single file below Saint Germain des Champs at the end of the houses and fields. Some of them try to reach the thick brambles that run along the wall made of flat stones placed on top of each other without cement. From time to time the sentry who is guarding them hits them on the head with his stick. It is the same sentry for everybody and the same place for prisoners of both sides. You go to Notre Dame de la Salette for Rogation days. It is in the country somewhere. You march two by two. You have to go through the whole town. You have navy blue uniforms on. You have white socks on. You have learned to march in the playground during gymnastics, you know how to make a right-angle turn, you have no trouble keeping in step. You have been ordered not to break ranks to let a car go by, so you pretend you are going to make way for them, you leave a big space in front of you until the car starts to drive through the column, and just at this moment you hurry forward so that the car is forced to stop and you are forced to go around it now to keep in line, and everybody starts to run to get around it in time, and there is a big mess, and Mother of the Infant Jesus runs along the rows too with her skirts flying out behind her to try and restore order. You are walking along a sunken road with hedges on either side. The sun is still low and there is dew on the grass. You see it shine in the places where the rays hit the ground at an angle, to the east it is pale green all new, in the clipped fields there are daisies buttercups dandelions, the violets have died you don't see them at the foot of the hedges, in the fields of tall grass there are budding daisies and big poppies. The blossoms have fallen from the trees you see them here and there yellowed or still fresh, lying on the damp ground. The pink that you see on the apple trees is from flowers that are still there, they are full of light green leaves, now in full bloom. Your feet are wet. Mass is held outdoors. You can look at the sky the whole time and the farms which look small because they are far away, you can look at the intricate design made by the hedges intersecting or running in parallel lines from one end of a field to another. On the nearest hedges you can see the black spines of the blackthorns, in places blackberries eglantines and other kinds of brambles form living hedges growing out of stones that have fallen from walls, stones that have caved in or even fallen on top of each other in dirty heaps. You pray that it will rain and that the grains will sprout well and that the fruits will grow. You pray that it will not rain hard enough to ruin the wheat and barley once they are high in the fields. You pray that there will be sunshine and that the fruits will become ripe and sweet. You pray that the sun will not be so burning hot that it will parch the fields and the fruits. The priest in his surplice blesses the water the bread the salt. You feel like tiptoeing away and going and walking on the bare grass down there. *Et je même i serai cevauchant l'auberc vestu lacié l'elme luisant l'escu au col et au costé le brant la lance el poing el prumier cief devant.* Mother of the Infant Jesus waits for Laurence Bouniol to find the page then asks her what this means. Laurence Bouniol says that it is Ermengart she tells how Ermengart at the French court abuses the French because of her son Guillaume who was treated like a dog, Laurence Bouniol says that it is right to come to her assistance for the aid of Orange. You see Ermengart on horseback all weighed down with armor helmet shield sword lance you wonder how she stays on the horse you see how it is at Agincourt horses with shins in steel guards on their backs, big human carcasses, their armor broken with limbs in all directions shields lances and swords, you see armies on the march riders rigid and when their helmets are pulled off their hair falls down in one piece it is Guibourc it is Ermengart, and *Se Dieu plaist aiderai mon enfant* then *Ke armée serai sor l'auferrant n'i a paien Sarrasin ni Persant se la cousieu de m'espée trenchant ne le convigne chaoir de l'auferrant.* Catherine Legrand stops drawing the Arabian eye of Guibourc or the snub nose of Guil-

laume. It is easier to begin the chapter with an initial.
You make the first letter very fancy, around it you
work lines in all colors it looks like illuminated
writing from a distance and you like the way it
looks. Mother of the Infant Jesus is pleased with it
too. When Mother of the Infant Jesus reads something she likes she stops and makes a kind of circle
with her mouth a silent O and in each of her eyes
there is an O just like it which means that this is
exactly what she was hoping to find and it pleases
her very much to admire something this way. She
has this habit of making an O over all the stories
in the books on the saints and she can't wait for
the sacred-history lesson when she can read stories
about saints out loud and keep stopping and making
an O. So you keep watching her and try to guess
when she will do it and at last she does it. Sometimes
you can even make her do it. This is why Catherine
Legrand doesn't play with anyone in the playground.
Nicole Marre comes up and asks her to play marbles.
Catherine Legrand refuses. She sees Marielle Balland
and Julienne Pont go by they run under the covered
playground where a game of Cops and Robbers is
going on. Noémie Mazat wants to play volley ball.
Catherine Legrand refuses pretending she didn't hear
them or barely heard them because it is very important that Mother of the Infant Jesus not see them
talking to her. Catherine Legrand is dying to go and
play anything at all but she won't go until Mother
of the Infant Jesus who is supervising play period

has noticed her standing all by herself against a tree and pretending to look at the ground or sitting and staring way off into space as far away as possible to where the eyes of the body can't see, as Mother of the Infant Jesus says, then Mother of the Infant Jesus will cross the yard in great strides making her robe fly out behind her, she will stop by the tree and bend over Catherine Legrand and ask her in a very sweet voice, What is the matter my child are you ill? and Catherine Legrand will shake her head no, and Mother of the Infant Jesus will say, But then what are you doing here? Catherine Legrand will throw back her head and say, I am thinking, Mother. Then if all goes well the O's will appear in Mother of the Infant Jesus' eyes which are the color of a squirrel. Perhaps after a short pause she will ask, And what are you thinking about, my dear? Catherine Legrand will put on a strange expression as if she is puzzled or bothered or distracted by her thoughts she will look at Mother of the Infant Jesus to see whether she can go ahead, and pausing a moment for effect she will whisper, I am thinking of God, I am thinking of . . . and she will press her lips together to keep from saying more and even if the two O's the ones in the eyes and the one on the mouth aren't on Mother of the Infant Jesus' face, anyway she will be right in the palm of your hand. Afterward when Mother of the Infant Jesus has gone off so as not to disturb Catherine Legrand she will wait for a while to be sure she can be seen staring into space, then she will seem to make a tremendous effort to come back to earth, she will walk with little steps still stiff and staring at the ground finally she will shake herself hard like a wet dog and then she can begin to run as hard as she can and join the others at last and begin to play with them at last. Mademoiselle Grangier says, Be seated Mesdemoiselles, still standing by the teacher's desk. Mademoiselle Grangier does not begin the Latin class right away, you can hear her giving Laurence Bouniol advice for the trip she is going to take to Italy saying that of course Laurence Bouniol must see the Roman ruins the Arch of Constantine the paintings of Pompeii and all that, then you hear Mademoiselle Grangier talking about Italian painting Il Pisanello, Masaccio, you hear that there is nothing more beautiful than Raphael and Mademoiselle Grangier says to read aloud what it says in Larousse, you stand up and say, Raphael, Rafaello Santi or Sanzio called Raphael, after a moment Mademoiselle Grangier says, Sit down. You sit down again. You finish the sentence, the inimitable painter of madonnas glowing with youth, freshness and chaste motherhood. When you have finished Mademoiselle Grangier looks at her watch and says it is time to do a little work. So you open your books and do some Latin. At the end of the row Valerie Borge is carving designs into the wood of her desk with Marielle Balland's pocketknife. After a moment Marielle Balland gets tired of not knowing what to do and watching Valerie Borge carve designs with her pocketknife so she tries to get the knife back, she bickers with Valerie Borge who doesn't want to give it back to her right away. Finally Valerie Borge throws it on the floor and Mademoiselle Grangier sees it and confiscates it, she will give it back at the end of the hour. Valerie Borge begins to draw in ink on pieces of paper. To show that she is mad at her Marielle Balland turns away from Valerie Borge who is in the same row so that she is all turned around and is obliged to twist her neck from time to time to look at Mademoiselle Grangier. Laurence Bouniol is really doing her Latin that is she is looking at Mademoiselle Grangier as if she wants to hear what she is saying. Mademoiselle Grangier sticks out her thick rouged lips, pulls them back, stretches them. When Mademoiselle Grangier opens her mouth you can see her palate. You are up to Hannibal before Capua. The battle of Trasimeno, for example. The story is told in the songs of Sidoine Appollinaire. He is believed to have been Bishop of Clermont and to have lived well before Charlemagne, well before the Roman churches, according to Saint Augustine, Tertullian and Suetonius. We assume that it was when in the History of the Franks Gregory of Tours talks about the Merovingians, that it was during an age when there were no paved roads on which to wander around the country. We may assume that the Roman roads are still new. In the Massif Central there are Roman roads like the one in the chestnut plantation which go all the way to Auvergne. They are unworn white slabs that have been placed end to end and are very flat on top.The carts with wooden wheels that go by jump from one stone to the next due to the lack of cement there is a space where they come together, they buckle even if you press the stones together hard, you see them go slowly by on the road between the trees, you see them disappear into the forest jolting and making a kind of rhythmic creaking because wood is rubbing against wood because the axle that carries the whole weight of the wagon is made of wood and the wheels that turn around it are made of wood and it doesn't do any good to oil it so it makes a sound like the peeping of a frightened bird and since there isn't any spring every time the wheel turns and bumps against the stone of the slab it sounds as though the wagon is about to fall to pieces. This is why wooden wagons do not often travel over Roman roads, this is why Sidoine Apollinaire writes stories about battles to pass the time in the mountains. You take notes: Merovingian dynasty, Meroveus, Childeric, Chilperic, Clovis and Clotaire. Mademoiselle Grangier bursts out laughing because she remembers that one day a student translated the passage about the lake of Trasimeno, The Romans dipped their behinds in the lake of Trasimeno, Mademoiselle Grangier stops laughing to explain what she is laughing about. Marguerite-Marie Le Monial is sitting next to Catherine Legrand because Nicole Marre is absent. Marguerite-Marie Le Monial bounces a ball against the wall when Mademoiselle Grangier turns toward the girls who are on the other side of the row. It is a little red ball made of sponge rubber. It makes the same sound as a fist when it hits the wall. When Mademoiselle Grangier who is standing in the aisle brings her head back to its normal position Marguerite-Marie Le Monial hides the ball in one of the pockets of her smock. When Mademoiselle Grangier is seated at her desk you can only scribble on your scratchpad, your desk, or the box of colored pencils Marguerite-Marie Le Monial draws a star with a tail on hers explaining to Catherine Legrand that it is a shooting star and now Marguerite-Marie Le Monial is writing something on the box opposite the star and she makes an arrow pointing to the star to show that what she just wrote refers to the drawing of the star that she made a little while ago. Catherine Legrand gets red when she reads that Catherine Legrand is as bright as a shooting star and sees that Marguerite-Marie Le Monial bursts out laughing. Mademoiselle Grangier comes down from the platform and pounces on the box of colored pencils to see what is written on it that is making Marguerite-Marie Le Monial laugh so hard. Mademoiselle Grangier tells Catherine Legrand that she has a high opinion of herself and Catherine Legrand gets very red again and says that it wasn't she who wrote that on the box of colored pencils and Mademoiselle Grangier bursts out laughing. Mother of the Infant Jesus is teaching the geology class. You make a cross section of the earth to show the most diverse aspects at the same time. First you establish the key: staggered lines to represent sedimentary layers, spaced dots to designate sandy regions and little spaced crosses to indicate crystalline rock and volcanic regions, you make a deep black with India ink for the volcanic rock itself, the places where volcanoes may become active again. You don't understand the difference between crystalline rock and volcanic rock. You ask Mother of the Infant Jesus whether it is necessary to distinguish between crystalline rock and volcanic rock since their composition and origin seem to be the same. Mother of the Infant Jesus says that in geology it is customary to distinguish between them perhaps because crystalline rock, although composed like lava of mineral, quartz and mica, has solidified at an earlier period, while volcanic rock is still magmatic and close to lava. Mother of the Infant Jesus says that you have only to look at obsidian it looks like black and shiny glass but it does not look very rigid it looks like a liquid that is holding still because of its weight. Mother of the Infant Jesus says that they are from different geological strata. On a vertical cross section you make a rough and simplified diagram of a region with its deep as well as its superficial layers. You work over the volcanic regions in which you see the gleam of obsidian, the less uniform basalt with green spots of silicate, in which you see that the light-colored trachyte threatens to spoil the nice black of the India ink

that you have saved for the basalt and obsidian while
the granite found in another geological layer must
be content with the white color which is supposed to
represent chalcedony or quartz or mica. When you
look at the sketch you have just made you tell yourself that Mother of the Infant Jesus is right about
volcanic rock. You can see very well how beginning
with harmless zones of sand and passing through
layers of sedimentary base you come to crystalline
rock and above all to the scene of the drama that
is the volcano, the black spot in the drawing, here
something moves, this is the place of greatest change,
this is the center of activity in the earth. If you
drove a tunnel through the earth from one pole to
the other or in a straight line from one point on the
equator to another, presumably on the surface you
would find a constellation of black cones the old
volcanoes would come to life again, then new ones
would burst forth at unknown points then there
would be nothing but a black and shiny magma, a
surface of barely chilled glass on the drawing. If
you were playing marbles with the spheres that are
in space you would put the earth with the agates
you would say it is the most beautiful, Guess what
it's made of, it's made of onyx. You look out the window at the clouds scudding across the sky. You will
have to light the lights you can't see a thing. You wish
you were in the garden for the first clap of thunder
to see the lightning between the trunks of the chestnut trees to wait for it to strike one, for it to wither

and become a little ball of fire bouncing on the ground like a tennis ball. The first drops land on your cheeks they feel as big as teacups. Mother of the Infant Jesus demands silence. She is sitting straight up in her chair and looking the pupils right in the eye one by one. Nobody seems to be paying attention. Marielle Balland is trying to catch a fly that is buzzing against the windowpane on her left. Mother of the Infant Jesus says, Marielle Balland, back to your seat, and she taps the wooden ruler against the wood of the desk. Marielle Balland sits down again. The fly goes back and forth along the pane bumping against it. Anne Gerlier is talking out loud to Denise Causse. Noémie Mazat is copying her mathematics homework over. The pupils at the back of the room are playing they are on a ship that is rolling and pitching, shoving each other with their shoulders until Marie-José Broux falls on her behind on the floor of the aisle. Then Mother of the Infant Jesus who is trying to obtain order without moving begins to yell, A little discipline Mesdemoiselles and Marie-José Broux, you will stay in on Sunday, I'm giving you a zero in deportment. When everybody is finally quiet Mother of the Infant Jesus says Marguerite-Marie Le Monial's mother is dead, let us pray, and Nicole Marre bursts out laughing and Mother of the Infant Jesus looks at her and she can't stop laughing so she takes her handkerchief and holds it in front of her face with both hands and laughs into it. Mother of the Infant Jesus tells her to leave the room and Nicole

Marre goes out with the handkerchief against her mouth. Mother of the Infant Jesus says that two pupils will go to the funeral and everyone raises her finger because it means that much less time to spend in class and Mother of the Infant Jesus says that Marielle Balland and Laurence Bouniol will go and that now you will all take your notebooks for dictation. Marguerite-Marie Le Monial takes off her black coat and hangs it on the coat rack in place of the smock which she slips on over her black dress. You see that she has black socks on. Catherine Legrand asks Nicole Marre to change places because she is going to ask Marguerite-Marie Le Monial to sit beside her. Marguerite-Marie Le Monial sits beside Catherine Legrand. Her black hair comes down to her shoulders. The skin of her face looks whiter than usual because all her clothes are black. Catherine Legrand doesn't know what to say to her. You see that at the end of the row Valerie Borge is hiding behind her arm and writing something. Mother of the Infant Jesus asks Valerie Borge what she is doing. Valerie Borge does not answer, she puts both arms on her notebook now to hide what is written there. When Mother of the Infant Jesus asks to see her notebook she shakes her head no and finally lays it down on her two arms which are stretched out on the table. Laurence Bouniol gets up and says, Mother it's poetry. But Valerie Borge presses her head even harder onto her arms and you can see that she is pressing them onto the notebook as hard as she can. If you pulled the notebook away from her you would tear it. Then Mother of the Infant Jesus speaks very gently to Valerie Borge and asks her to bring her her notebook. You can't tell whether Valerie Borge hears what Mother of the Infant Jesus is saying to her. Anyway she turns her face toward the wall so that she can't see anyone. Her hair falls over her shoulders and partly covers her arms. If someone pulled it back she would have to lift her head then and look toward them. So Catherine Legrand gets up and says, *Et déjà devant moi les campagnes se peignent* and then Valerie Borge lifts her head and looks over at Catherine Legrand who looks her right in the eyes and says, *Du safran que le jour apporte de la mer.* Laurence Bouniol is reading over Valerie Borge's shoulder and she gets up and says, But that's what she wrote in her notebook. Mother of the Infant Jesus looks first at Catherine Legrand and then at Valerie Borge. At last she says to Valerie Borge, That is very nice poetry, Valerie Borge, but it isn't yours. Valerie Borge gets up holding the notebook against her and runs out of the room. Marguerite-Marie Le Monial pokes Catherine Legrand with her elbow and asks, What is it? Catherine Legrand doesn't answer. Marguerite-Marie Le Monial keeps on asking, What is it, if you tell me I'll give you something and she looks in her desk for something to give Catherine Legrand moving books and notebooks rummaging in a clutter of objects staying behind the desk top which rests on her head. Mother of the Infant Jesus raps in front of her with the wooden ruler. Marguerite-Marie Le Monial pulls out her head and lowers the desk at the same time. Mother of the Infant Jesus is saying, What are you doing behind your desk? So Marguerite-Marie Le Monial doesn't find anything to give Catherine Legrand but this doesn't keep her from hitting Catherine Legrand with her elbow on either the arm the elbow or the forearm so that Catherine Legrand has to pull it back each time and say, Leave me alone. Mother of the Infant Jesus is quizzing Noémie Mazat on the Songs of Guillaume d'Orange. Mother of the Infant Jesus asks her to read and explain the passage about Ermengart, the one you read together during the last class. But this time you don't feel like reading along with Noémie Mazat, *Et je même i serai cevauchant l'auberc vestu lacié l'elme luisant la lance el poing el prumier cief devant et se Dieu plaist aiderai mon enfant*, this time you know it all by heart, the Saracens and Persians thrown down their heads cut off, you can't say that Ermengart still has anything new to tell you. There would have to be something else to make you pay attention now. Here and there you try hard to make Mother of the Infant Jesus understand this by whispering wiggling and opening and closing your desks. But it doesn't do any good. Mother of the Infant Jesus raps in front of her with the ruler stopping what she is saying, looking at the pupils and waiting stiffly in her seat for the noise to stop so that the class is a hundred times slower than if you hadn't moved. Apparently you will be on Guillaume d'Orange until the end of the year. Catherine Legrand leafs through the reader, she passes Chrétien de Troyes and Marie de France one after the other she has already read their poems which are in the anthology, she stops at those of Charles d'Orléans which she hasn't read. There are only two of them. Catherine Legrand reads them several times and picks out two verses of the second poem which she copies into her notebook *Tout a part moy en mon penser m'enclos et fait chasteaulz en Espaigne et en France*. This way Catherine Legrand can refer to them when she likes and even say them aloud when she is alone. Valerie Borge has not returned to her seat, she is walking along the acacia path or she is in the vegetable garden with Mother of Saint Nicholas, they are picking gooseberries black currants red currants. Valerie Borge watches the sunlight showing through the seedy pulps. The lightest ones are the color of vin d'Anjou, all of them are translucent. The ones Valerie Borge eats are very warm on her tongue, Mother of Saint Nicholas puts hers into the fold she has made in her apron and looks at Valerie Borge and laughs. Mother of the Infant Jesus asks Marielle Balland to repeat what was just said. Marielle Balland starts on the bench she is sitting on and looks around her with frightened eyes. You can hear a pin drop. Mother of the Infant Jesus says, I'm waiting. Then as nothing happens Mother of the Infant Jesus asks Marielle Balland to give the meaning of the words *auferrant auberc elme brant*, et cetera. When you go up the marble stairs you see No admission written everywhere, underneath the signs there are barriers so you won't try to go that way. You are having a retreat. You aren't allowed to talk. You are taken to the convent which you see at the end of the garden. There are nuns there whom you don't know because they stay behind the walls. You can see their garden when you walk through the park by the acacia path but you aren't allowed to go into it. There is a stone niche with a Gallo-Roman statue that was found in the ground of the garden. When you walk quietly over to the niche you can see that it is a woman standing with her arms outstretched. Her legs are in motion. The pattern made by the legs and thighs is more important than the rest of the body, this is because they are long, they give the woman a monumental quality, she seems to get smaller toward the top as if her head is lost among the stars. And yet it is only a tiny statue from the Gallo-Roman cemetery. You are in a room with tables and wicker chairs and big windows through which you see the trees stir. The floor is marble as it is everywhere you have been in the convent. You have notebooks in which you may write whatever you like. Mother of the Infant Jesus will not look at them. You are sitting in the chairs. You can walk around the room as long as you don't make any noise. You can do handwork, you can mend your underwear you can draw you can make things out of wood with knives. It is like a long play period except you have to whisper, you can also talk to someone when you want to by writing what you want to say in the notebook and waiting for the answer to be written there too. You're not being supervised because Mother of the Infant Jesus said, I trust you I hope you will deserve it. This is what you do, you don't talk out loud, you don't start running around the room, you don't move the furniture around, you are very happy to be on your own, so if someone goes by in the corridor and listens she won't hear any noise. You can read. You have a passage from Pascal on some typewritten sheets. You read it. It begins like this, That man contemplates Nature entire in her high and full majesty, it is called Disproportion of Man, Mother Superior handed it out saying that there wouldn't be any commentary on it, I ask you to give it your full attention, I suggest that you read it often and if you take down in your notebooks whatever comes into your mind when you read this passage it will be a good exercise for you. You also have at your disposal some saints' lives: the life of Saint Francis of Assisi, the life of Saint Catherine of Siena, the life of Saint Theresa of Avila, the life of Saint Amand, the life of Saint Estèphes, the life of Saint Enimie, the lives of still other saints but you don't read them. Catherine Legrand opens the notebook and writes on the first page, *Tout a part moy en mon penser m'enclos.* Farther down Catherine Legrand makes drawings. She tries to draw a picture of the opoponax, but it doesn't come out right, so Catherine Legrand decides to make words instead of lines. So she writes in capital letters in the middle of the top of the second page OPOPONAX and a colon and then, can change its shape. You can't describe it because it never has the same form. Kingdom, neither animal nor vegetable nor mineral, in other words indeterminate. Humor, variable, it is not advisable to frequent the opoponax. Catherine Legrand goes to the next line where she writes again in capitals, Summary of the manifestations of the opoponax, after that she goes to the next line and writes, General examples then colon then, You are sitting at your desk. Mother of the Infant Jesus or Mademoiselle Grangier or Mother of Saint Jules or Mother of Saint Hippolytus raps several times with her ruler to tell you to close your desk. You have to close it. But you can't. There is something in the way. You can put the top down to a certain point but after that it refuses to go any further, it doesn't do any good to look you don't see anything, or to force it, the top won't go any further. It's the opoponax. So Mother of the Infant Jesus or Mademoiselle Grangier or Mother of Saint Jules or Mother of Saint Hippolytus gets mad, thinking you're doing it on purpose. You can't force it. You have to pretend you don't notice anything, crush a book or two if you have to to close the desk, it won't be the same height as the others but it won't necessarily be noticed. You're sitting in front of the table in your room or you're in the dormitory and you're trying to go to sleep. You are disturbed by the sound of a leaking faucet in the washbowl of the bathroom or dressing room. You get up and turn the tap. Good. It's stopped. But then it begins all over again and this time the drop falls so slowly it drives you crazy, it trickles, it hisses, and when it has fallen it is immediately followed by another so that there is a double splash. This is the work of the opoponax. And it's also him when you feel something run over your face when you're lying in bed in the dark. Or when you happen to turn around suddenly in a room where you are alone and you catch sight of a dark shape just slipping away, just vanishing. Or you are looking at yourself in the mirror and it covers your face like a mist. You must not give up you must stare at the mirror as if you didn't notice anything and it will go away. Catherine Legrand closes her notebook because Nicole Marre comes and looks over her shoulder to read what she is writing. Catherine Legrand goes to the chapel which is across the hall from the room you are in. When you look at the door of the chapel you think you are going into a room exactly like the one you just left but suddenly you are in a place where the pink ocher mauve stained-glass windows soften the light, where the walls gleam, where gold gleams on the altar which is a single stone. Arum lilies roses amaryllis are in vases on the floor. Laurence Bouniol is kneeling in front of the grille of the choir. In the last pew Anne Gerlier and Marie Démone are showing each other pictures. Man needs animals to help him in his work. Catherine Legrand adds in her head, And to fill his stomach. For example goats sheep cows pigs. This is what it says in the book. You are in geography class. You write in your notebook, Cultivation and Breeding, this is the title. The little cows that Uncle yokes to help him with his work don't like it very much, you can see them shake the reins, shake the rails, break into a gallop on the rutted road while Uncle yells something at them to calm them down but it doesn't work they run as fast as they can the cart is all shaken, at a certain point one of the pair slows down moves her back flicks both sides of her stomach with her tail and stops while the other continues to pull on her side because she has not run down yet but in the end she is forced to stop because now she has the other cow to pull besides Uncle and the cart. So the cow who is on the side of the embankment begins to graze while the other moos and Uncle pulls on her rein calls her name gets mad pleads with her but doesn't hit her because he loves her. Then there is the pig hanging upside down in the barn but that's not at Uncle's he is hung up by his hind feet, he doesn't look as if he likes it too much either he squeals while his carotid is cut and the blood flows into the basins it goes on and on you can hear him scream, pull on his throat as hard as he can croaks come out of him, he makes his lungs pop but this is good this helps, the man who is killing him is glad, this forces the last drop of blood out and the pig doesn't stop screaming until he hasn't a drop left, after that the flesh is good, well aerated and all. In the photographs in the book on the first page of this chapter you see fields and in the background, mountains, when you read the caption you see that it is Greece. On the second page there are more fields but there aren't any mountains in the background and in the fields there are white cows that get smaller and smaller, in the background there are dots beside the farmhouse which has two roofs a red one and a black one. Underneath it says Plains of Charolais. The third page is nothing but a photograph, it must be an aerial view because unless you were on a very high mountain you would never see that much of the countryside. In the foreground there are lots of trees, behind them a broken wall runs diagonally all the way across the page, it looks like the Great Wall of China. The wall is open in the middle to leave a passage you see the road that runs off on the other side up to a huge house with several buildings around it. In the back there are a lot of houses but they are so small that even when you screw up your eyes you can't tell whether they have windows. You can see that the white marks behind these last houses also represent houses but seen from so far away or so fast or both that they look like a white paste spread at the foot of the cobalt hills unless it is the fault of the camera. Mother of the Infant Jesus is talking about the life of the nomads giving the Peuls the Tuaregs the Hebrews of the Bible as examples. They have camels whose feet they have to take care of in the evening because of the sharp stones and thorns and remove their calluses. In the photograph in the middle of the chapter you see some big shepherds following some big sheep. These are Turks. They don't have any camels, they don't need them, they stay on the grassy plateaus, they don't have to go far to pasture their sheep and these sheep are lucky, because sometimes you see sheep who have to push the stones aside with their noses to find the twigs that they eat, dry twigs, sumac or juniper. Mother of the Infant Jesus is talking about the shifting of flocks and crossbreeding. Marguerite-Marie Le Monial is making little balls out of blotting paper, she is stuffing them into a round hole in the floor, she is cramming them in with her ruler, packing them tightly until she can put new ones in, telling Catherine Legrand that she is making a hole in the ceiling of the room below which is the one where you go to Dominical. Catherine Legrand tells her to use erasers because this will add more weight and she hands her hers dropping it on the floor by accident and you hear it roll on the floor of the classroom. So Catherine Legrand says that she is going to go look for it without Mother of the Infant Jesus noticing, for this reason she slides the length of her bench until she is kneeling on the floor and creeps under the desks on all fours passing between Julienne Pont and Marie Démone whose legs and knees she sees then going behind between Nicole Marre and Anne Gerlier whose legs and knees she also sees. You hear Mother of the Infant Jesus say, Where has Catherine Legrand gone? so Catherine Legrand sticks up her head with her hair in her face between Nicole Marre and Anne Gerlier who begin to laugh very loud and Mother of the Infant Jesus asks, What are you doing there? and Marguerite-Marie Le Monial gets up saying, She is looking for her eraser Mother. You are at four-thirty play period. Marie-José Broux Anne-Marie Brunet Julienne Pont are playing marbles. The holes that you have carefully made in the place where the yard is flattest stay there from one play period to the next. They are well worn. The distances that separate them are not the result of chance, they follow precise rules, the courts formed by the straight lines leading from one hole to the next having been drawn in proportion to one another. For example, the distance from the first hole you see to the second is half that from the second to the third, the lines of direction form angles, so that there are overlapping geometric figures, triangles placed end to end, quadrilaterals, pentagons, hexagons, and other polygons whose names you don't know on the ground. You roll the marbles along the ground and when you hit an opponent's marble you have taken one of his towns, that is, one of the holes, away from him so you make a circle around that hole with the stick to show that the town has fallen. You can also take the town by surprise, by rolling the marble into one of your opponent's holes but it's more difficult you can't do it on the first try at least hardly ever and your opponent has plenty of time to see the maneuver and to defend himself. Denise Causse and Catherine Legrand are walking side by side and talking. Denise Causse is telling Catherine Legrand that there is a ghost in the dormitory you can't see him but he taps on the metal springs of Mother of Saint Sylvester's bed with Mother of Saint Sylvester's slipper before she has gone to bed. Denise Causse says that the ghost does it every evening that it was Valerie Borge who first told her about it, Denise Causse says that ever since Valerie Borge told her about it she always listens and that she hears it quite clearly now and that the proof that it's true is that it isn't a regular sound, Denise Causse says that you ought to try to catch him but that Valerie Borge doesn't agree. Catherine Legrand asks Denise Causse whether it's true that Sophie Rieux grinds her teeth in her sleep. Denise Causse says that from the bed she sleeps in she can't hear her but that Anne-Marie Brunet whose bed is next to Sophie Rieux's hears her grinding her teeth, she even says it keeps her awake because it would be one thing if she just ground her teeth but every so often she clicks them loudly and it's always just as Anne-Marie Brunet is dropping off to sleep and it scares her. Denise Causse tells Catherine Legrand that Anne-Marie Brunet often asks Sophie Rieux to stop making the noise but Sophie Rieux says that she can't help it, that she doesn't do it on purpose and that she doesn't even know she's doing it. Denise Causse walks beside Catherine Legrand without speaking. Suddenly she tells Catherine Legrand that if she will promise not to tell anyone she will tell her something. Catherine Legrand promises not to tell a soul. So Denise Causse leads her to a place where no one can hear them. It is beyond the yard with the statue.

There are Jerusalem artichoke flowers as tall as Catherine Legrand and Denise Causse. When you run your finger along the stalks they are rough because of the thousands of little thorns on them, the stalks are velvety with white spots. Denise Causse tears off a leaf and begins to roll it between her fingers saying, Did you know that Valerie Borge writes poetry? Catherine Legrand doesn't say anything. There is a moment of silence. Catherine Legrand asks, Have you read any of it? Denise Causse says, No she won't let me but you won't tell her I told you, will you, you mustn't tell her. You see Anne-Marie Brunet walk across the yard to go and ring the bell for the end of play period. So you walk slowly back to the front steps crossing both yards because this is where you line up to go to the study room. You are in the chapel. All the nuns from the convent in back of the garden are either in the stalls or around Mother of Saint Ignatius of Antioch who is at the organ. The nuns of the convent in back of the garden, the nuns of the school and even Mother Superior have all lowered their veils in front of their faces. Even if you study their silhouettes you can't tell who they are, you can't recognize their voices, sometimes they are very high then they go down. What you are hearing are plain songs. *Suscipat te Christus qui vocavit te.* In front of the grille of the choir there is a coffin laid on a trestle over which the black burial cloth has been draped, it fits over the coffin so that two white crosses show on each side. Tassels hang from the four corners. The corpse that is inside it is that of a cloistered nun whom you don't know. You are at the mass for the dead. The priest is wearing a black chasuble over the alb and a black stole around his neck. Mother of Saint Barnabas is kneeling in the choir serving mass and since she has to see what she is doing she hasn't put her veil down in front of her face. You don't say *Et introibo ad altare Dei* and I go to God who is my joy because it is a mass for a dead person. The priest is kneeling at the foot of the altar saying *Confiteor Deo omnipotenti*. Mother of Saint Thomas of Aquinas who works in the kitchen is at this mass. Mother of Saint Nicholas who takes care of the garden is here too. The mass is sung slowly so that each prayer which is normally very short is repeated several times today and drawn out by the singing. The regular mass lasts half an hour. It seems as if this one is going to last an hour and a half. For this reason the pupils were allowed to eat breakfast before mass which they don't usually do. Mother Superior was afraid that you might pass out from the smell of the incense on an empty stomach. You have seen the priest put his arms apart put them together walk up to the altar kiss the stone. He has gone to the right of the altar to read the *Introit*. You have heard them sing the *Kyrie eleison*. Three times *Kyrie eleison*, three times *Christe eleison*, three more times *Kyrie eleison*. There is no *Gloria* because of the dead nun in the coffin. The priest kisses the altar stone again, he turns around, the altar is behind him, he looks at the congregation and puts his arms apart and puts them together again. He says a prayer in Latin and you say Amen after he says *Per omnia saecula saeculorum.* Mother of Saint John the Baptist reads the Epistle out loud in French, it is Saint Paul's letter to the Thessalonians, But we would not have you, brethren, ignorant, concerning those who are asleep, lest you should grieve, even as others who have no hope. Then you hear several songs, *Requiem aeternam dona eis, dies irae.* The *Dies irae* takes up two pages in the missal. It is the first time you have heard it. Mother of Saint John the Baptist gets up again to read the gospel. Mother of Saint John the Baptist says, The gospel according to Saint John, Martha therefore said unto Jesus, Lord, if thou hadst been here, my brother would not have died. There is no *Credo.* The priest turns around again and puts his arms apart then you hear them sing the offertory. The priest has washed his hands, there are more prayers and now you hear them sing the *Sanctus* which is included in the ceremony in spite of the dead nun, so you say *Hosanna in excelsis.* The priest waits until the singing is finished then he says a prayer in Latin about the bread then about the wine which he holds up in turn while Mother of Saint Barnabas rings the bell for you to bow your head. Catherine Legrand sees that Valerie Borge is kneeling in front of her, the nape of her neck shows through her hair which falls on either side of her face because of its weight, her hair is divided by a center part that is approximately straight from the roots to the ends. Catherine Legrand sees that it is because Valerie Borge's head is bent that her hair falls this way. It is the first time she has seen Valerie Borge's neck uncovered and she realizes that she doesn't like long hair, that it doesn't look good on top of clothes, that it only looks good when it is pulled forward by its own weight to reveal the long blonde nape of Valerie Borge. In fact it is those little hairs that she has and the down that make her seem blonde because Valerie Borge's hair isn't blonde, you can see that it has a bronze cast. When Valerie Borge's head is up again her hair stays on her chest on each side, still divided by the movement she made when she flung it forward. Catherine Legrand sees that Valerie Borge is beginning to make reliefs on the page of her missal of all the change she has in her pockets. She begins by putting one coin on the right-hand page of the missal then she folds the left-hand page over it and holds it as tightly as possible over the coin until you can see the pattern, pressing with her thumb and being very careful not to make holes in the paper. When she has done this, keeping the circle of paper thus formed over the coin the whole time, she runs her pencil, whose point is rounded, over it. The result is that she has the profile on the coin on the page of her missal right in the middle of the canon, just below the red initial. She traces another and another and when she has run out of coins she uses the same ones over, the page of the missal is completely covered with the impressions of coins. And Valerie Borge doesn't choose just one side of the coin as when you play Heads or Tails, she puts the paper on the obverse and when she has obtained the head or effigy she turns the coin over to get the impression of the reverse. With coins whose impressions are almost flat she puts black lead on her thumb and rubs the coin gently until the design appears on the page of the missal which is laid on top of it. You see that with all this the mass has gotten as far as communion, which means that you see Mother Superior Mother of Saint John of God Mother of Saint Paul of the Cross Mother of Saint Alexander Mother of Saint John the Baptist walk down the center aisle with veils over their faces. Valerie Borge slams the missal shut so no one will see the impression of coins made with lead right in the middle of the *Preface* and *Agnus Dei* of the mass for the dead. You hear coins fall to the floor but not one nun turns her head toward you, anyway they couldn't see anything with their veils down. The nuns go to the communion table single file. After Mother of Saint John the Baptist go Mother of Saint Bonaventura Mother of Saint Apollinaire Mother of Saint Hippolytus Mother of Saint Nicholas Mother of Saint Gregory Mother of the Infant Jesus Mother of Saint Jules Mother of Saint Francis of Assisi Mother of Saint Thomas Aquinas Mother of Saint Sylvester Mother of Saint Ignatius of Antioch. You recognize them when they pass the pews from their voices and their silhouettes. You hear them saying in a shrill and monotonous voice, *Domine, non sum dignus*. The organ stops playing because Mother of Saint Ignatius of Antioch is in the center aisle under her veil. The nuns are kneeling side by side in front of the choir, each time the priest approaches one of them with the host saying *corpus domini nostri*, et cetera, you see her lift up her veil and hold it in front of her face with both hands so the priest can reach her mouth. The pupils do not take communion. You don't know the nuns of the convent in back of the garden who are now going down the center aisle single file. Valerie Borge has succeeded in retrieving her coins by sliding them with her foot until they are right under her then bending down and picking them up. Valerie Borge tosses her head back to the left to get her hair out of her face, she runs her hand and arm under it to keep it from getting caught in the collar of her coat. The pupils are now lined up in the center aisle. You go up to the coffin and when your turn comes you take the aspergillum which Mother of Saint Barnabas standing on the step of the choir is holding in the pail of holy water and you make the sign of the cross over the coffin and the organ starts to play again and you hear the choir sing *Libera me domine de morte aeterna*, and you hear the passage *Requiem aeternam dona eis domine et lux perpetua luceat eis* repeated several times and you turn away from the coffin and go toward the door and you see the line of pupils going up the aisle the other way. Mother of Saint Gregory is supervising shop. Marie-José Broux Laurence Bouniol

Julienne Pont are making billfolds. On the flattened strip of leather which will form the flaps you put a strip of silk the same color as the leather but the surface of the piece of cloth is smaller so you fold the edges of the strip of leather over the piece of cloth, then you begin sewing them together, you fold the leather in half. Two strips of decreasing size, both made of silk and only bound with leather, will be added to the first, and a fourth strip smaller than the others will come last which will be of leather lined with cloth, this will be the inside of the billfold, when it is open the leather side of the last strip will show. Marielle Balland Sophie Rieux Nicole Marre Marguerite-Marie Le Monial Denise Causse are doing bookbinding. Nicole Marre is fitting the headband to the top of the book she is working on as she sews. Marielle Balland who is just starting is working on her leather, trimming it with the cutter, Mother of Saint Gregory is standing beside Marielle Balland to keep an eye on her because you can give yourself a deep gash with the cutter and even cut off a piece of your finger. Mother of Saint Gregory has her hands in front of her, she keeps putting them out toward Marielle Balland to take the cutter away from her but she doesn't do it except when Marielle Balland makes a hole in the leather to show her that she isn't holding it right. Marguerite-Marie Le Monial has almost finished, the book has been in the press, she is gluing the endpapers. The spine of Marguerite-Marie Le Monial's book is smooth because Mother of Saint

Gregory doesn't want to take up bands just yet and since Mother of Saint Gregory doesn't want to take up quarter binding just yet either, Marguerite-Marie Le Monial's book is all leather, Mother of Saint Gregory will have to make an exception for Denise Causse because she hasn't enough leather and she will be forced to leave the boards of the book bare. Valerie Borge is polishing some pebbles that have one rounded end which gives them the shape of an egg, she does it by rubbing them against each other which makes a very unpleasant noise which grates whenever a grain comes loose from a stone, whenever it is caught in the motion and rolled and worn between two stones. Catherine Legrand decides to make a herbarium, she will begin with the flowers she picked during one-thirty play period. While you are waiting for tissue paper which won't damage them when they are dry you can glue them into your drawing pad with gummed paper. You don't have very many: some broom, two roses and a lily. You have to put atlases and dictionaries on top of them to flatten them out. When you look at them you decide you don't want to crush them. Catherine Legrand asks Mother of Saint Gregory whether she can put captions under the plants she has. Mother of Saint Gregory says, That's a good idea since you don't know what to do. So Catherine Legrand asks Valerie Borge to take off a piece of mica for her from the block of schist she has in her desk. Valerie Borge passes her the stone telling her to do it herself. Catherine Legrand does it with Marielle Balland's pocketknife. The first pieces she gets crumble into dust. Catherine Legrand cuts deeper sticking the point of the knife into the particles of quartz which hold the particles of mica in place. By using the knife as a lever Catherine Legrand manages to get a small flake of mica whole. Marielle Balland watches her do it and begins to fume because the blade of the knife gets chipped in one place. Catherine Legrand fastens the flake of mica next to the broom with gummed paper. Then she writes in ink below it, *E tu lenta ginestra che di silve odorate queste campagne dispogliate adorni.* The piece of mica is there to illustrate the last line. It is a passage from a poem which Catherine Legrand translated this morning and which she now understands. In the same notebook she finds a passage that Mother of Saint Hippolytus gave as an exercise and she starts to copy it in the blank space beneath the two roses, *La mer et le ciel attirent aux terrasses de marbre la foule des jeunes et fortes roses.* Catherine Legrand likes the effect except that her handwriting isn't pretty and she can't make a straight line. But there isn't anything for the lily. Catherine Legrand remembers a poem that Nicole Marre sometimes recites because her father taught it to her. So Catherine Legrand goes and sits beside Nicole Marre but Nicole Marre isn't in a good mood because of the headband which isn't going on right and whose threads are getting tangled, the reds with the greens. Catherine Legrand repeats the same thing to her four times, finally Nicole Marre tells her to go to hell. When Catherine Legrand is back in her seat again she hears Nicole Marre start to sing in a loud voice to tease her, *Sur l'onde calme et noire où dorment les étoiles la blanche Ophélia flotte comme un grand lys*, so she quickly writes the words she hears while she still remembers them, but she doesn't listen to what comes after *un grand lys*. On the first page of her drawing pad Catherine Legrand writes again in big letters in black ink, *Tout a part moy en mon penser m'enclos et fais chasteaulz en Espaigne et en France.* Laurence Bouniol and Anne-Marie Brunet pass Catherine Legrand's herbarium to Valerie Borge as they were asked to do. Valerie Borge puts the pebbles down on the table and picks up the notebook so that you stop hearing the sound of one pebble rubbing against another. Valerie Borge reads what Catherine Legrand has written in the notebook which she has in her hands. The writing is so big that you can almost read the words from where Catherine Legrand is sitting. Valerie Borge closes the notebook and passes it to Anne-Marie Brunet and Laurence Bouniol before Catherine Legrand has time to tell her to keep it that she has made it for her. Noémie Mazat whom Mother of Saint Jules has brought with her to repair the electric fixture in the parlor comes into the classroom. You are at four-thirty play period. Denise Causse comes down the front steps with a pile of sandwiches and comes toward Catherine Legrand who is under the covered playground who pretends not to see her who begins to run and jumps over the wall dividing the two yards and goes to the back where the statue is in front of a thuja bed. Marie Démone and Anne Gerlier are sitting behind the statue eating their sandwiches. You see them opening their mouths over their bread which is sliced too thickly for the size of their jaws. Valerie Borge is not with them. Catherine Legrand asks Marie Démone and Anne Gerlier if they have seen Valerie Borge. Marie Démone and Anne Gerlier say no but that they saw Véronique Legrand fall down while playing ball, that Mother of the Infant Jesus who supervises play period took her to the infirmary. Catherine Legrand runs across the yard to go to the infirmary. She passes the nuns' private room the door to which is open, you can see them sitting side by side at a table. Catherine Legrand runs up the stairs, she is told to enter when she knocks and when you are inside you see that Véronique Legrand is sitting on a chair, that Mother of Saint Francis of Assisi is crouching in front of her, that there is a basin of water on the floor. There is a big wound in Véronique Legrand's knee, Mother of Saint Francis of Assisi is cleaning it with a piece of cotton but you can see that it immediately gets red from the blood that flows. Mother of the Infant Jesus standing by the open window shakes her head as she watches, saying, The poor thing it must hurt but Véronique Legrand starts to smile and Catherine Legrand bends down and kisses her. Mother of the Infant Jesus tells Catherine Legrand, Good, you will look after her and she goes away. There is nobody lying in the bed of the infirmary. The white cover is pulled tight so that Catherine Legrand doesn't dare sit on it. Mother of Saint Francis of Assisi stands up and says, Now this will hurt a little my dear but it is necessary, hold onto the chair, you see her pour alcohol at a ninety-degree angle onto a clean piece of cotton and apply it to the knee of Véronique Legrand who does not hold onto the chair but leans over to watch Mother of Saint Francis of Assisi dab at her knee. After this mercurochrome is put on and a gauze bandage is wrapped around the knee several times and tied in back. Mother of Saint Francis of Assisi helps Véronique Legrand to her feet, then she puts her hand behind her head and pushes her toward the door asking whether she feels all right and telling her, We'll have to clean it again this evening. Catherine Legrand and Véronique Legrand close the door of the infirmary. Catherine Legrand takes Véronique Legrand's hand. Véronique Legrand keeps leaning over to look at her bandage and she doesn't dare put her foot down normally because of the knee which hurts when she bends it, so she walks with her leg out and limps. Catherine Legrand asks her if she wants to stay with her during play period but Véronique Legrand says she would rather go and play with the girls in her own class. So Catherine Legrand lets go of her hand. Just then Catherine Legrand meets Sophie Rieux and asks her if she has seen Valerie Borge. She is told that Valerie Borge has been seen walking on the acacia path, that she is crazy that she will get a zero in deportment. Denise Causse who has waited for her under the covered playground sees Catherine Legrand leave the playground and walk along the paths of the park where you aren't allowed to go before she has time to catch up with her and now she doesn't dare follow

her. Catherine Legrand searches all the groves one
after the other. Valerie Borge isn't there. On the way
to the vegetable garden you find Valerie Borge lying
on the ground in the arbor. She is reading a novel
that Catherine Legrand doesn't know. She half rises
leaning on one arm and looks at Catherine Legrand
who doesn't know what to do. In the end she sits
down on the ground beside Valerie Borge who smiles
at her and begins reading again. Valerie Borge's black
smock is rumpled and covered with twigs bits of
straw dust. When you look up you can see the sky
between the leaves of the rose bushes trailing between
the white or red flowers. Catherine Legrand picks a
rose and begins to play with it unconsciously so that
Valerie Borge stops reading for a moment and says,
What are you doing? so Catherine Legrand drops
the rose throwing the two or three petals that remain
in her hands into Valerie Borge's face. Valerie Borge
shakes herself and laughs and lies down on her back
and keeps reading the book which she holds with
both hands in front of her eyes. Catherine Legrand
writes in the dirt with a stick, she digs out the shape
of each letter carefully so you can read everything,
she writes all the words of *Plaisant repos plein de
tranquillité continuez toutes les nuits mon songe.*
Valerie Borge is sitting beside her now you can hear
her deciphering out loud what is written in the dirt,
you can see her ear behind which her hair is secured,
you hear her say, But you didn't make up those lines,
you don't hear her say that she found them in her
study desk in Catherine Legrand's handwriting.

The town you are in is in mourning because of the bishop who is dead. You walk through the streets. There are crowds in the center of town where the bishop's house is. When you lean over the ramparts you look at the gillyflowers between the disjointed stones. The stems of those you manage to pick make a yellow liquid on your fingers when they are crushed. Some people use it to cure warts. You will go to the funeral. You will walk in a procession. There will be other girls from other schools in navy blue uniforms like the one you have. You won't have any class that day. And the night before you will go to pray in the big room where the body is lying in state, which has become a funeral chamber. You have to wait at the door because the room is full. You hear the murmur of the people who are inside, it makes a sound like a lamentation. You don't see people crying. In the adjoining rooms and in the big room you go into it's like a hive, there are people coming in, people milling around, you are shoved against the high black catafalque draped in black with a flat top, it looks like a Merovingian altar with lateral steps to get to the pulpit which is visible from everywhere, dominating the flock of faithful crowding around the bas-reliefs. But on the platform of the catafalque you can't see anything except the black of the hanging cloth. You breathe with difficulty in a red penumbra. This is because of the flowers placed everywhere in high-necked vases, in amphoras, in bowls, in big pots. There are clusters, bells, trumpets, flowers with pistils, flowers with heavy blossoms, with overlapping petals. It might be the cannas with their broad garnet-spotted leaves, the foxgloves, the lobelias, the madders, the amaranths, all bell-shaped flowers, simple or in clusters, tall, medium, short, it might be the peonies whose petals are already beginning to fall, the roses wilting or budding, the tall dahlias, the gladioli, the stiff and pointed tulips some of which resemble red lilies, the orangey-red daisies and their larger version the Chinese asters, it might be the stemless flowers here and there in bowls, impatience or anemones. The flames of the candles tremble in the breezes created by people coming and going. You don't know if there is to be a ceremony. You don't know what the two black-robed priests who are leaning toward each other on the other side of the catafalque are saying to each other. You walk very slowly behind Mother of Saint John of God. You see that she is holding in her hands the wooden rosary which is normally in the folds of her robe. The wax of the candles gets warm, melts, gives off a smell. When you close your eyes there is red behind your eyelids. There is a red screen between the crowd and the catafalque, a haze that rises and falls, that lifts in places, disappears and reappears with the movements of the bodies. You wait while long mournful Latin sentences emerge from some breast, that of a clergyman, his hands crossed on a breviary and his head leaning to one side, or a peasant woman dressed in black with a big bouquet of eglantine or poppies clutched against her, and are taken up by all mouths, spoken, sung, like weeping. A ray of sunlight falls onto the carpet below the drapes whose edges don't reach to the floor. When, after walking around the room, walking around the catafalque without touching it, when after leaving slowly following the direction of the crowd you find yourself outside again, you squint in the sunlight, you pause a little to one side on the stone steps to let the crowd go by, to look at the well, the red stones and the curb, the paving stones of the yard and the bunches of purple clematis on the walls. You drink coffee standing in the refectory. You put the cups down on the white tables. You hear the metal of the spoons clink against the cups, the marble of the tables or the stone of the floor. You drink scalding hot coffee to clear your voice. You see Mother of Saint Jules standing by the table, Mother of the Infant Jesus goes to the dumbwaiter and takes the tray which she brings herself. Through the open door you hear Mother Superior go by talking with Mother of Saint Ignatius of Antioch. You are in the street standing two by two in a long line. You don't move. Mother of the Infant Jesus Mother of Saint John of God Mother of Saint Jules Mother Superior Mother of Saint Ignatius of Antioch Mother of Saint Gregory go back and forth along the rows in the gutter. You see their big capes fly back with a single movement. The cathedral is on the other side of the square with its great bare façade, without portal or tympanum, only the rose window in the top third which for the moment looks very small. You are going to walk across the square, walk beside the cathedral, pass the little statues of the Gallo-Roman idol sculpted along the lateral wall. You can't move because of the crowd walking in the same direction. You take a few steps and stop. The big door of the cathedral which is on the side is now open. The stones are of red sandstone, when you look up you can see them all the way up forming a mass. The cathedral looks like a fortress. You hear voices singing in Latin long before you get to the door. You drag your feet on the ground. You stand in place.

You walk in slowly. You are surrounded by the chill of the cathedral, by voices which are unevenly dispersed. You hear them echoing everywhere starting from the choir, spreading through the transept, lingering in the nave, bumping into the big columns. The wall opposite the choir which closes off the cathedral at the parvis sends them back so that the music of the choir which bursts forth as if from a single voice immediately falls apart, is absorbed as if by air pockets or echoes which repeat and multiply it all over the cathedral. The acoustics are bad. You can hear the voices struggling to be heard. The cathedral is full of people trying to move forward. There are peasant men in smocks, peasant women in straw hats and black dresses. There are merchants from the town, schoolchildren, clergymen, those who also came who are not in the choir serving mass but mingling with the crowd. There is the same smell there is in squares on fair days. Mother of the Infant Jesus says that mass is being said by a bishop. On the left you pass the ambulatory which is full of people standing crowded against each other, the chairs have been taken away, some people are going up the stairs of the confessionals to see into the choir, others are trying to balance themselves on the toruses and plinths of the columns, but since they are too big around for you to stay on by hugging them, they fall off. You are moving up the side aisle you can't see anything because of the enormous shafts of the pillars. The ones that are cylindrical are just as enormous as those with engaged columns. You have stopped opposite one of the lateral chapels. Over the altar you see a fragment of bas relief hanging from two cords. It is a figure in a gloriole composed of two tangential curves. He seems to be sitting on the upper semicircle and his legs are in front of the second semicircle his feet are on a kind of ladder, one of the arms is almost at right angles, bent at the elbow, the thumb and index finger are also bent, the other arm is holding a book upright on the thigh, you can see the closed hand holding the edge of the book with the fingers extending over the sides. The head is cut off at an angle so that you can only see the beard the mouth and the beginning of an eye. The folds of the robe curve in over the shoulders, make a circle on the breast where the fabric seems laid on as it does over the stomach whose bulge you can see. Clusters of folds fall almost vertically over the bare feet. Along the wall of the chapel next to the ground you see the reclining statue of a bishop with the miter on his head, the crozier is laid beside him on the pedestal. You picture to yourself the officiants in the choir, the deacons and the bishop dressed in dalmatics. You imagine that the bishop goes from time to time and sits in the pulpit, that a deacon hands him the crozier and the miter which he puts on his head. The other deacons go back and forth in front of the altar, several have incense boxes, several have censers, there are some who carry cruets, the *manutergium*, there are some who move the canons, one of them takes the asperges, you see him in front of the altar.

You assume that there aren't any choirboys. You see Mother of the Infant Jesus stand on tiptoe several times to try to see what is happening in front of the main altar, you don't know if she can see anything, all you can see is that she finally comes down on her heels again, perhaps because she is tired. Marie-Jośe Broux and Sophie Rieux are whispering together. Catherine Legrand is next to Nicole Marre. Catherine Legrand and Nicole Marre aren't talking. Nicole Marre leans her head back to look at the capitals. Catherine Legrand is looking at the stone of the floor and the bases of the columns, she can't go any higher than the cornices because it makes your head spin to put it back and look at the arches, the curves, the ribs or the rose windows. A crowd of people cut Mother of the Infant Jesus Marie-Jośe Broux Sophie Rieux Catherine Legrand Nicole Marre off from the rest of the boarding school in front and back. You don't try to get back to them, you remain motionless waiting for the mass to continue. You are too far away to follow the words said in Latin, at times you hear the shrill and distant sound of bells, you don't know how far along it is. At the elevation you bowed a few rows at a time, the gesture has reached the back of the cathedral and the people standing in the side aisles in the chapels in all the corners, until at last everybody is bowed. At a certain moment you feel stirrings in the crowd, breezes go by and bend the flames of the candles burning in the chapels, and you realize that the crowd has imperceptibly started to move again.

There is no point in steering you must let yourself be carried along so you move without the sensation of walking toward the wall of the cathedral where the main entrance has not been opened as you might expect but where you can see where you are, that is inside the cathedral, that a semicircular apse follows it, just opposite the first apse and forming a second choir, this one unused and sticking out into the main nave. The interior hemicycle does not affect the external architecture of the cathedral since behind the apse the outside wall appears a bare fortified wall, a plane surface perpendicular to the ground. You turn a right angle to go back up the nave, the light falls onto the pillars, they are light gray, they gleam like tempered steel, you move forward, you hear the organ whose sound is carried differently in different parts of the cathedral, now softened, now magnified. When Catherine Legrand turns around she sees behind her Valerie Borge's hair which is immediately hidden by a movement from Anne-Marie Brunet, Valerie Borge's mouth which is immediately hidden by the shoulder of Anne-Marie Brunet who is walking in front of her. Catherine Legrand tries to get out of the crowd to stand aside and wait for Anne-Marie Brunet Valerie Borge Marie Démone to go by but she is shoved from behind, she is pushed, she has to go forward, Mother of the Infant Jesus motions to her to look ahead of her, to keep walking, so Catherine Legrand loses sight of Anne-Marie Brunet and Valerie Borge. Véronique Legrand moves around on the stage according to certain directions which you don't know, she comes and goes back and forth, she is describing a diagonal which becomes the tangent of a curve or a circle. You don't see a smile on her face, she is holding a bow in her left hand and dancing. The crescent she has in her hair and whose horns are sticking up has a metallic glitter in the light of the footlights and the spotlights. You wonder if Véronique Legrand is one of the followers of Artemis but after a moment it is clear that this is Artemis herself advancing and treading the ground with an impatient foot. Besides you look only at her on the stage and the movements of the girls who surround her seem to be determined by hers and merely to set the scene for her, you see around her movements which she stops with a wave of her hand as, motionless and her loins taut, she draws the bow with all her strength. You don't see a smile on her face. You wait for her to shout and jump or give a violent kick or thrust of the shoulders or neck and dash off stage, letting her hair, which is loose on her shoulders, fly against her cheeks as she runs. But Véronique Legrand does not shout she obeys the different measures of the music. From the right side from which she returns she pauses with her feet together stiff in a leap in the center of the stage where the girls who surround her bow while she watches them motionless. It is Mother Superior's birthday. You are sitting on the benches in the Dominical room. You are talking and whispering while waiting for the monitor at the door of the room to announce Mother Superior's arrival. The curtain on the stage is lowered. You hear noises coming from the wings, sometimes from those on the right, more often from those on the left because this is how you get to the stage. It sounds like furniture being moved or scenery or other heavy props. You hear people going up and down the wooden steps that go from the room to the stage. At a certain point you see a figure appear at the center closing of the curtains, raise the panels of the two curtains to hide her body, then disappear almost immediately. On the third bench to the right of the aisle there are Marielle Balland Nicole Marre Marguerite-Marie Le Monial Valerie Borge Laurence Bouniol Catherine Legrand. Catherine Legrand is standing in the aisle waiting for the pupils who are in front of her to sit down on the bench. She will sit beside Valerie Borge because Valerie Borge has been in front of her in the line ever since it formed to go down the aisle. Catherine Legrand stands in the aisle waiting but lo and behold Laurence Bouniol who was originally seated between Marielle Balland and Nicole Marre gets up passing in front of everybody and places herself between Valerie Borge and Catherine Legrand so that now Catherine Legrand is sitting next to Laurence Bouniol, whom Valerie Borge begins to smile at and talk to. The monitor beside the door keeps closing and opening it to pass the time until Mother of Saint Alexander comes and tells her to stop. So when you turn around you see her holding the door with one hand very stiff along the jamb.

Suddenly the monitor begins to call There she is, and Mother of Saint Alexander Mother of the Infant Jesus Mother of Saint Ignatius of Antioch Mother of Saint Hippolytus Mother of Saint Apollinaire motion with their hands, and Mademoiselle Magne begins to play the piano. Mother Superior walks briskly into the room, the beads of her rosary clink steadily and you can see the soles of her shoes disappear alternately beneath the bottom of her robe which is lifted the veil drawn back the whole garment moved by her small and rapid steps. Mother Superior who walks without seeming to move her body redoubles her speed when she comes to the first ten benches and tries not to walk in time with the march for Mademoiselle Magne is pounding the piano harder and harder because the tune you hear is that of a wedding march. Véronique Legrand stiff in the center of the stage presents a narrow body, all of a piece. You have the impression that she is making an effort to stand still and you wait for her to start running again. You see that her hair which stays close to her head has gleams of steel in its blond color, that Mother Superior is smiling in the red armchair that has been placed in the first row leaving a space between her seat and the first benches. The pupils run around Véronique Legrand, come back to her, stretch their legs as they run, go faster and faster until they are galloping on the stage, you see what look like lifted manes, you wait for shouts with which those of Véronique Legrand would mingle because she has joined them now, she has leaped from one end of the stage to the other in a single stride and you see Artemis and her followers disappear into the trees each of them lifting her body high but you see that Véronique Legrand is roused even more than her attendants by the movement of the dance, you see her head and shoulders above the others so that she is the last figure you see among the trees, Véronique Legrand as if borne away by the followers of Artemis. Today again you hear the song that makes you cry. Mother Superior leans toward Mother of the Infant Jesus who is sitting on a chair next to her. You see her whisper something in her ear. When the curtain is raised the scene that you know by heart is repeated for the nth time. You see a knight with blond curls kneeling, it is one of the older pupils, her name is Dominique Vurse. She is sitting on her heels and singing a poem of love. *Douce figure avec toutes les vertus je saurai par vous supporter des injures car vous êtes le terme de toutes les folies.* The lady who listens to him, seated on a low chair and dressed in a gown that covers her knees, might be Beatrice of Provence. You see the troubadour exit and reenter to indicate the passage of time, when he returns for the third time he doesn't sing a poem of love, he throws himself on the ground in front of the lady who has black hair and whom you don't recognize, pleading with her, kissing her hands which she pulls back then walks offstage quickly trailing her gown on the floor and you see the knight weeping on the ground with his head in his arms. When the two characters are together again, Dominique Vurse begins to sing again and you can see her teeth under her parted lips and her hair stirs. You understand that she is saying farewell to the lady who may be Beatrice of Provence, you see the lady take off the ring that she wears on her index finger and give it to Dominique Vurse, and Dominique Vurse receive it in her two joined and upraised hands. You see Dominique Vurse one more time but you don't recognize her right away, you realize it is she when you see something shine under the scapular because she is dressed as a monk. Then you see enacted how she came to be separated from the ring that the lady who may be Beatrice of Provence gave her, why it is that she must obey the prior of the convent. You understand the song that she sang just now when she asked the lady for a souvenir of herself. Mother of Saint John of God has Marie-José Broux recite the rule on the use of the reflexive in Latin and asks her first to give an example and then to explain the rule in terms of the Latin sentence. Marie-José Broux is in front of the blackboard playing with the chalk, from time to time she turns toward the class and then she turns back to the board where she hasn't written anything yet. You are bored sitting on the bench, you are a fish because the walls are like the inside of an aquarium, you slide against them whether you are standing or sitting, the green makes the light thicker something like translucent, the eyes slip through, the fish that you are is getting bigger and bigger, he is ready to swallow the benches one by one, to grow, to swallow everything else, including the pupils and even Mother of Saint John of God. When he is as big as the room he will wiggle with all his might, his tail will hit the ceiling, he will press his scales against the windows, you will hear the house tremble. It is as if there were no one in the classroom, no one anywhere and wherever you go you bump into green into glass into all kinds of things you can't go through so you have to stay there without moving until you hear voices saying, What are you doing, what are you doing, you aren't paying attention, until you hear laughter you don't know why when for example Mother of Saint Jules says You are dreaming and this makes everybody happy and you can see the mouths parting over the teeth. What are you to do during the hours that pass in immobility the hours when you don't even know what you are doing? What can you do? Meanwhile the clouds go by behind the windowpanes and even when there is no wind so that they don't seem to be moving they go faster than you do motionless on the bench because those aren't the same ones you see in the place where you looked a little while ago which seem to be standing still. So since you are doing Latin you try to make up a tune for *lento me torquet amore*, the line that Dominique Vurse made Catherine Legrand read from her book following it with her finger until you knew it by heart.

You look at Valerie Borge who is staring into space and who is far away, you don't know where. You ask Valerie Borge in a whisper where she is but she doesn't hear so you try to answer for her, you say that she is in the darkness of a night without end, you say that she is riding a wild horse that is black white gray the color doesn't matter since you can't see it, you say that her unbound hair is streaming in the wind you see her with her fingers in the mane and her knees bare, all covered with sweat, you see Valerie Borge going she knows not where, her mouth open, her teeth bared. You tell yourself that she may be elsewhere, drawn by movements of stars she drifts, you see her disappear, she is a sparkling frost that you watch whirling round and round, she is traveling toward a galaxy. When you get tired of imagining where Valerie Borge is like this you see that Mother of Saint John of God is up to the cases when you replace the reflexive with *is ea id*, that the Latin class hasn't made any progress, that Valerie Borge is still in the same position staring into space, that you don't know what to do, all you can do is drum on the table with your fingers in time to the tune you have in your head for *lento me torquet amore*, you say I can't stand it but you don't know. You are at four-thirty play period. You see Véronique Legrand run under the covered playground with Nicole Gerlier and some other girls whose names you don't know. You are with Nicole Marre. You are waiting for the boarders to come out of the refectory.

Through the door which is open onto the front steps you see Mother of the Infant Jesus Mother of Saint Hippolytus Mother of Saint Jules walking in the hall not going in the same direction. You see Sophie Rieux Anne-Marie Brunet and Denise Causse come down the steps trying not to spill the pile of sandwiches they are holding in their hands because as they walk they are biting into the top sandwich, the one on top of the pile, half stopping, first they stick out their mouths and then their whole heads you watch them drop crumbs of bread bits of pâté bits of ham bits of cheese or jam which run over their fingers which they will lick when they have finished everything else. You see apples or oranges in their gaping pockets. You watch Sophie Rieux Anne-Marie Brunet Denise Causse go over to the little wall where they sit down and put their sandwiches on their laps except for the ones they are eating. Then you go behind the statue with Nicole Marre. You draw on the ground with a stick. You make lopsided circles triangles squares rectangles, you don't feel like writing your name or anyone else's name on the ground. You can't make figures or heads or houses, you keep making more circles more triangles more squares more rectangles, they overlap, the dust rises, your hands are dirty, you begin to spit on the ground to keep the dust from rising and getting on your hands, it takes a lot of spit to make mud you don't have enough, the place where you spit is hardly visible hardly darker than any place else with outlines in filigree and a bit of slime on the edges. You see that Nicole Marre has gone behind the thujas, you can hear her running rustling leaves breaking stems, you get up to see what she is doing, she is catching a butterfly that is flying over the dahlias. She is holding her handkerchief out in front of her. It looks too rumpled to be good for anything, it is stiff because it is dirty, maybe Nicole Marre wiped her shoes with it. She has on beige wool socks that aren't pulled up, you can see that they are in a heap around her ankles. Nicole Marre is sitting with the butterfly in her hands which she is keeping closed. She grabs it, lets it go, she opens her hands a crack. She holds the body with one hand with the other she presses one of the wings to her knee, she wipes this wing gently until it has no more color the spots disappear first it is like a powder that he has stuck to his wings, then she wipes the background and finally you can see through the butterfly's wing, it looks like a transparent leaf with the veins. The butterfly fluttered both wings then just one now he isn't moving any more, maybe Nicole Marre hit him on the head by accident, anyway now she is working on the other wing and the butterfly is as ugly as anything. So Nicole Marre tears off first one wing then the other, the body falls to the ground, Nicole Marre tries to do the way you do with chestnut leaves when you pull off everything between the veins with the tips of your fingers and end up with a leaf skeleton but it doesn't work because the membrane of the butterfly's wing breaks into little pieces that crumble into dust. Nicole Marre is trying to get rid of the pieces of butterfly that are still on her fingers she stands up looks for the fallen body and stamps on it until it disappears into the ground. You see that Marie Démone Anne-Marie Brunet Denise Causse Anne Gerlier Julienne Pont Valerie Borge are together. Nicole Marre and Catherine Legrand walk across the yard to go and see Marie Démone Anne-Marie Brunet Denise Causse Anne Gerlier Julienne Pont Valerie Borge. You hear them asking Valerie Borge to tell the rest of the story she began last play period. Valerie Borge is playing with the ends of Anne-Marie Brunet's belt. Valerie Borge says, No I don't feel like it. Anne-Marie Brunet pulls her aside to tell her something. Marie Démone Denise Causse Anne Gerlier Julienne Pont are trying to remember the facts of the first part of the story. Nicole Marre jumps up beside them on the stone bench gets down again jumps up jumps down again. You see that Anne-Marie Brunet is taller than Valerie Borge. They are walking back and forth side by side. Valerie Borge isn't talking. Anne-Marie Brunet is talking and gesturing you see her put her hands into the pockets of her smock and pull on it with her fists, turn around making a hole in the ground with her heel, and dig her fists deeper and deeper into her pockets. Catherine Legrand goes to the back of the yard where Noémie Mazat is at the net reaching for the ball, you see her rise as if without effort she is always smashing the ball so that neither Suzanne Prat nor Nathalie Deleu on the other side of the net can return it even when they fall flat on their faces diving after the ball which they lose which goes away somewhere or other which doesn't go back to Noémie Mazat's side of the net. *Je suis maître de moi comme de l'univers je le suis, je veux l'être. O siècles, O mémoire.* Mademoiselle Doullier leans her head back, her left arm is extended beside her while with her right hand she picks up the book that was on the table and drops it again. Now her hands are side by side. You are in French class. Mademoiselle Doullier is talking about the sublime, she likes Corneille and Saint Vincent de Paul. Mademoiselle Doullier says that there is a certain discipline, the control of the passions. Nicole Marre is next to Catherine Legrand. She is pulling on her braids, she takes off the rubber bands that secure them, she begins to undo the last turns making the hair spiral then she attaches them to her chest with one of the rubber bands which she hooks to the button of her smock. Mademoiselle Doullier raps the ruler very hard against the table. Nicole Marre gives a cry and stands up. Mademoiselle Doullier tells her to sit down and pay attention to what she is saying. You learn that passions don't mean just weaknesses of character or things you endure as its etymology indicates. You understand that Mademoiselle Doullier is referring primarily to the meaning of sacrifice and suffering that the word may have for example the passion of Christ or the passion of

Joan, this becomes very complex you understand that carried to its extreme passion may become active for example a passion for learning a passion for duty so that from something endured it becomes a force that overcomes will and reason. It is in this sense that Corneille's characters have a passion for duty. Nicole Marre begins to cough loudly beside Catherine Legrand. All of a sudden Nicole Marre cannot resist imitating the sound of a trumpet which she does well, you hear a trumpet play distinctly three or four times followed by the sound of somebody laughing then you see Nicole Marre snickering behind her desk and Mademoiselle get up, you hear her high heels click on the platform, she is beside Nicole Marre, she is shaking her, she makes her leave the room she is still red when she goes and sits behind her desk again. Mademoiselle Doullier begins to talk about Augustus again saying that if he said Let us be friends, Cinna, you are my guest, it was not a political move for example to avoid further conspiracies, if Augustus pardoned Cinna it was not out of expediency, Mademoiselle Doullier says that Augustus pardons Cinna because leniency has become a duty for him, that he goes so far as to absolve Maximus and *tutti quanti. Conservez à jamais ma dernière victoire.* The benches are empty except the one Nicole Marre and Mademoiselle Doullier are sitting on. Mademoiselle Doullier has one arm behind Nicole Marre on the back of the bench. They are going over the French lesson. As you have just eaten Mademoiselle Doullier is trying as hard as she can to hold back the gas that rises from her stomach to her mouth so that she touches her stomach with her hand, she rubs it, she massages it as far up as her throat but from time to time gas escapes and bursts on her lips, it only lasts a moment, you know that Mademoiselle Doullier is having trouble digesting her meal. All of a sudden Nicole Marre asks her, Why do you belch all the time? Then you hear in the classroom the cries of Mademoiselle Doullier who pulls Nicole Marre off the bench throws her on the floor and starts kicking her in the stomach with her high-heeled shoes. You are walking down the hill toward the bridge by the highway. Snakes slip out of the bramble bushes that grow out of the flat stones at the edges of the fields. The stones are warm. It is noon. The Roman reflection of the arches of the bridge are motionless on the water. You see them as you walk across. You see that the surface of the water is pulled along by an underlying movement without seeming to change itself, you notice it as you cross the bridge because the leaves you threw into the water as you went by are now far away they turn until they reach the break which you can just see at the place where the mill wheel sucks the water. The road is an extension of the bridge you are on, another road cuts across the first one at right angles and runs along the river. You leave the bridge and follow the river. Dust from the road raised by cars trucks or tractors covers the hedges. As you walk you hear the sound of poplar leaves stirring endlessly. When you look up there is a kind of flashing in the trees, it looks like the metal foil you wrap around bean or pea poles to scare away the birds. You see snakes or lizards running away. Right after the bridge the river has a loop in which there is a sandy beach. This is where you are going. Véronique Legrand and Catherine Legrand have strainers which they have made themselves, making their edges slightly raised, with a surface two hands across, they are adequate for your purposes. You are playing gold-washers. You dip the strainer into the water as far as you can, if it doesn't touch the bottom it will be empty when you bring it back up, so you put the strainer in as far as the arm will reach until the edges scrape the sand. You find grains of gold mixed with sand. Véronique Legrand brings her strainer out of the water, everything in it is covered with mud, so she walks bent over holding the strainer under the water so its contents will be washed. Then Véronique Legrand squats down to pick out the grains of gold. The gold of the rivers is deposited on the bottom on beds of sand or carried down along the falls to the bodies of water that are in front of the dams. All you have to do is separate it from the water, when you have finished you put it in a handkerchief which you stretch as hard as you can to remove its many wrinkles. It is mixed with flakes of mica which glitter in the thick sand they are mostly transparent although tinged with ocher. Catherine Legrand says that you will set up a giant crucible here beside the river. Catherine Legrand marks off with a stick the area to be covered by the crucible. Véronique Legrand is shaking her strainer, the sandy water that comes out of it runs down her legs, you can see dried traces of sand on the tops of her thighs because a moment ago the whole strainer spilled onto Véronique Legrand. Now she holds it away from her a little when she shakes it. What you see along her legs are splashes. Prospecting should not be limited to the banks so you see Véronique Legrand take off her shoes and socks and wade into the river walking straight ahead as if to cross it. Véronique Legrand holds the strainer in the air with her right hand waiting to dip it into the water. You hear the cries she utters when she loses her balance on the edge of a hole or stubs her toe on a stone. Véronique Legrand goes back and forth between the water and the bank where she sorts the grains of gold from the sand. Véronique Legrand catches the grains that are visible on the surface with her fingernails then when they are all gone she shakes the strainer so others will come to the surface, there isn't any more room in the handkerchief, besides the grains break there so Véronique Legrand goes and gets some flat stones and lays them end to end to form a table on the ground and pours the grains onto it. While she is in the water a breeze sweeps the table clean. Catherine Legrand adds more crucibles making diagrams of their bases in the sand, deciding on various shapes for them.

It is agreed that their triangular tops will all be the same height, making a conical forest in which the liquid gold will circulate. Back at the flat stones Véronique Legrand is not happy about the disappearance of the ocher, black or cloudy grains of gold. Véronique Legrand tries to find them by getting down and looking all around the stones but the wind has driven the weightless particles far away and there isn't a trace of them. Véronique Legrand finds a clump of trees growing together and thus forming a platform sheltered from the wind at their bases. You see that the edges of her clothing get wet when she stoops down to deposit the grains of gold. They say that for the purest gold, river gold, you don't need crucibles. River gold doesn't need to undergo transformations so if you must build something here it would be better to make a giant screen, a kind of winnowing machine into whose hopper Véronique Legrand and Catherine Legrand could throw the sand containing the gold in shovelfuls. You are at four-thirty play period. Laurence Bouniol Julienne Pont Marielle Balland Noémie Mazat Marguerite-Marie Le Monial Nicole Marre are playing ball in the covered playground. Denise Causse is walking beside Catherine Legrand with her pile of sandwiches. You see that in the yard with the statue Anne-Marie Brunet Valerie Borge Sophie Rieux Marie Démone Marie-José Broux are having tea. Anne-Marie Brunet is sitting next to Valerie Borge. You see that Anne-Marie Brunet is peeling an orange, she removes the pieces of white skin clinging to the sections which she separates, you see her cut them up one at a time, you see her put each orange section into Valerie Borge's open mouth. Then you see Valerie Borge take Anne-Marie Brunet's index finger, you see her suck it, and turn it against her tongue to lick off the traces of pulp or orange juice. Sophie Rieux is scraping the apple which she has just dropped in the dust by mistake and whose bitten part is blackish with a thuja branch stripped of its bark. Anne-Marie Brunet Valerie Borge Sophie Rieux Marie Démone Marie-José Broux have finished their tea. You hear a laugh from Marie Démone whom Sophie Rieux is carrying piggyback, you see her stand on the bench where Sophie Rieux puts her down. Valerie Borge now has around her Sophie Rieux Marie-José Broux and Anne-Marie Brunet who is nearest to her, Marie Démone who is just behind her. Valerie Borge is talking. Her hair is pulled behind her head and falls down her back. Nobody talks when she does. Marie Démone is half off the bench, her right leg is bent she is leaning on the heel of the foot which is still on the edge of the bench, Marie Démone has two purple spots in her white cheeks, these are the eyes whose eyelids you can't see. Valerie Borge is moving her hands as she talks. You can't hear what she is saying. Denise Causse has finished eating her sandwiches. You have stopped because she is cracking nuts with her feet. Valerie Borge is untying the red muslin scarf which is tightly knotted around her neck and which shows above the collar of her black smock. Catherine Legrand wanders around the playground and wherever she is she never stops looking at Valerie Borge even when she is walking or nodding or shaking her head in answer to what Denise Causse is saying. Valerie Borge throws her head back when she talks, you can see the curve of her bare neck, you can see the swell of her throat at the place where the thyroid gland is. Valerie Borge opens her lips to make certain syllables so you can see her teeth and her pink gums. Now you see her lower her eyelids over her eyes and stop talking. Anne-Marie Brunet begins to laugh. Catherine Legrand sees her take Valerie Borge's hand and shake it in her two closed hands. Valerie Borge is talking again. She is looking straight ahead half at the ground of the garden, half at nothing. Valerie Borge isn't looking at Catherine Legrand. So Catherine Legrand approaches the group Valerie Borge is in followed by Denise Causse. You hear Valerie Borge say, The body that Misan and Rellure put in the chimney before they left falls into the middle of the room scattering the fire. Its face is black, it smells bad. Orphire and Rennie both jump to their feet screaming, getting pale, running around the room to escape. Valerie Borge doesn't notice that Denise Causse and Catherine Legrand have joined the group that surrounds her. Catherine Legrand pokes the ground with her shoes, digs her hands into the pockets of her smock, in one of them there is a handkerchief which Catherine Legrand begins to play with, bringing it out of the pocket and pulling it this way and that until the fabric gives way. Valerie Borge continues the story she is telling saying that when Orphire and Rennie came back into the room they did not find the body, that the people who are with them search the room and look in the chimney in vain. Catherine Legrand tells Denise Causse that she is going to look for Véronique Legrand but she doesn't go away. Catherine Legrand looks at Valerie Borge who doesn't look at her. Play period passes this way with Anne-Marie Brunet Sophie Rieux Marie Démone Marie-José Broux around Valerie Borge listening to her with Catherine Legrand telling Denise Causse over and over that she is going to look for Véronique Legrand but not going until finally Catherine Legrand leaves the group and crosses the yard to go and find Véronique Legrand by the covered playground and you see when you turn part way around that Anne-Marie Brunet has let go of Valerie Borge's hand and is crossing the yard to go and ring the bell. I am the opoponax. You must not provoke him all the time the way you do. If you have trouble combing your hair in the morning you mustn't be surprised. He is everywhere. He is in your hair. He is under your pillow when you go to sleep. Tonight he will make you itch all over so badly that you won't be able to go to sleep. When dawn comes behind the window tomorrow morning you will be able to see the opoponax sitting on the window sill. You will write to him and put the letter behind the piano in the study room. I am the opoponax. Valerie Borge turns the piece of paper she has just found in her desk in all directions. The writing is strange, full of circles and sharp angles, you can hardly read it. You see that it is written in vermilion ink. Mademoiselle Caylus looks in Valerie Borge's direction. Catherine Legrand who is seated two desks away in the left-hand row looks at Valerie Borge. Catherine Legrand looks at the piece of paper covered with red writing which Valerie Borge is holding in her hands and which you can see from all over the study room. Maybe Valerie Borge will get up, maybe Valerie Borge will take the piece of paper which she found in her desk to Mademoiselle Caylus. Mademoiselle Caylus has her hair pulled back in a braided bun. Mademoiselle Caylus wears metal-rimmed glasses. There isn't a sound in the room when it is Mademoiselle Caylus who is supervising study period. Everyone is afraid of her, you don't know why, but even though you have never heard her raise her voice Sophie Rieux Anne Gerlier Marie Démone and the others say that Mademoiselle Caylus is a nasty bitch. Catherine Legrand looks at Valerie Borge who is holding the piece of paper covered with red ink in her hands. She has to get rid of it, she has to do something with it, because you can see that Mademoiselle Caylus is shifting around in her chair, Mademoiselle Caylus isn't taking her eyes off Valerie Borge.

Catherine Legrand sees that Mademoiselle Caylus is
looking at Valerie Borge in spite of the reflection
which makes the lenses of her glasses shine and
keeps you from seeing her eyes clearly. Maybe
Valerie Borge will get up and take the piece of paper
she found in her desk to Mademoiselle Caylus. Valerie Borge looks up. Valerie Borge quickly puts the
piece of paper she has in her hands into a school
book which she puts into the open satchel hanging
from the back of the bench behind her. Valerie Borge
is keeping the notes you send her even though at
last Dominical Mother Superior said that private cor-
respondences are grounds for dismissal. Mademoiselle
Caylus turns her head away. Catherine Legrand looks
at Dominique Vurse who is sitting in the right-hand
row two desks beyond Valerie Borge. Dominique
Vurse has her left arm resting on the open Gaffiot.
Dominique Vurse is writing in her scratch pad. Her
hair bounces from time to time when she stops
writing. The curls are short leaving the nape of
her neck bare, from the front she looks like Antinoüs
du Belvédère, so that you stare at her with the
kind of golden light that she has all over her face.
You see Valerie Borge looking for something behind
her in the satchel. It is the opoponax paper, she keeps
turning it over, she starts to read it. Mademoiselle
Caylus is looking at Valerie Borge. Even allowing
for the elevation of her desk, though, it is impossible
for her to see the piece of paper Valerie Borge is
reading. The edge of it is wedged into the edge of

a book, on top of the book are the dictionary of the French language and the Gaffiot. Mademoiselle Caylus moves on her chair. You see that she is starting to get up which takes her a while because she has a bad leg, you see her stand up and come down the steps of the platform. Valerie Borge looks up again. Valerie Borge sees that Mademoiselle Caylus is coming down the center aisle toward her as fast as she can. Valerie Borge hurriedly puts the piece of paper into the satchel behind her and puts her scratch pad on the table. Mademoiselle Caylus is walking toward Valerie Borge. Mademoiselle Caylus will ask Valerie Borge to give her the paper she was reading. Mademoiselle Caylus stops beside Valerie Borge and begins to look at her, to look at the desk the books and Valerie Borge. Valerie Borge waits with her uncapped fountain pen in her hand. Mademoiselle Caylus stays there for a moment looking at Valerie Borge. Mademoiselle Caylus returns to her desk, you see her walk with difficulty up the center aisle. Catherine Legrand feels sick to her stomach so she gets up and asks permission to leave. You are walking through the tall grass repeating verses that you found in the text book to yourself, *La nature t'attend dans un silence austère l'herbe élève à tes pieds son nuage des soirs.* The sun strikes the tops of the grasses at an angle, you see its rays go through, the grass is lighted from beneath, you can see the ocher shadows or the spaces between the stalks, between the heads, sometimes even between the sheaths that form them. There are blankets of light along the ground. The grass and flowers are getting damp as if water were rising. There is a smell. Catherine Legrand doesn't know the names of the weeds that you see caught in the last light like this. Most of them are of indeterminate species. You see some that are long and tall, the elements that make up their heads look braided, they are hard between your teeth. Some are feathery like oats except that the sheaths containing the grain are smaller more widely spaced and more numerous. You see some that have downy tufts. Others are pink. There is plain grass. There are grains that are completely flat, there are compound umbels. When you run the grass hits your bare legs. Catherine Legrand's lips are bloody from the grasses she pulled up while she ran without looking at them, their edges are sharp, they have hairs a lighter green than the rest on both sides, they are so small that you have to hold the grass right in front of your face to see them. Catherine Legrand begins shouting her name with all her might. You can hear Catherine Legrand, her voice carries, you can hear it on the hills, people will rise up and move, on the hills an army will be on the march and will come toward the cry which has been heard far and wide. Catherine Legrand begins shouting other names, Marguerite-Marie Le Monial Anne-Marie Brunet Sophie Rieux drawing out the syllables modulating them shouting the same name several times. Catherine Legrand begins

shouting the names of pupils in her class. Several
times Catherine Legrand shouts the names of the
pupils in her class but she doesn't shout the name
of Valerie Borge. The people on the hills have lain
down again. Catherine Legrand begins to run she
jumps over the grasses so they won't cut her legs.
Somebody once told Catherine Legrand that if she
jumps above the surface of the ground, that if she
can just stay in the air a certain length of time and
if the earth turns beneath her during this time, she
won't fall back in the same place. It's one way to
travel. Catherine Legrand jumps as high as she can
and tries to keep herself up with her fists. Up there
like that you are Gulliver or Goliath but you fall
back in the same place, maybe it's because the earth
doesn't turn fast enough. Catherine Legrand walks
normally again. The poppies are shapeless, some of
them are still in the sun, there is a red haze around
them, the daisies don't hold their heads the same
way, some are crossways at different angles, some are
vertical, the field is all white with them. The end of
the field which Catherine Legrand is reaching is
mowed. The grass which has been cut today is
standing in green piles in which you can see flowers
that haven't faded yet. Farther on there are piles
of dry grass. You lie on the ground with your head
resting on the pile of hay. Your cheeks are scraped
by the edges of the grass, pricked by their stems
which the scythe has cut off. The heads are dry
but the bodies and branches are resting on the damp

ground. You hear a dog bark. You don't hear a sound. The vegetation is motionless. The air is still warm. You see that the sky is empty of clouds except at the horizon where the sun is disappearing. Catherine Legrand is drunk from the smell of the grass, she rolls on the ground from one pile to another, she sinks her head into them and inhales. You don't see a house. The cows the heifers the bulls aren't in the fields, they are inside. You don't hear any mooing. Everything is motionless. The light is receding from the grass. A few patches of the field are still struck by it which makes the rest of the field around them look black. So Catherine Legrand gets up and begins to run toward the sun which looks enormous, which looks very close. Catherine Legrand runs through the field, she feels her heart beat, her heart is beating so hard in her chest that you can hear it, you can feel it knocking against your ribs, Catherine Legrand runs toward the sun, her heart rocks back and forth through her body, the blood beats at her temples, in front of her eyes, it's like a fog, the sun begins to beat, you can see the contractions of the blood beaten back, sucked in, passing across the sun, you hear the sun begin to beat harder than your heart on the horizon, back and forth, through Catherine Legrand's body, you hear it, the noise is so loud it explodes in your head, so loud that your heart and the sun explode that Catherine Legrand falls on the ground with her face in the grass. When Catherine Legrand turns over there is no more sun in the sky, her clothes are soaked from the grass or sweat, then a breeze comes up, you see the trees stir, you feel it in the clipped grass, you hear it. There isn't anyone in the big aisle in the dormitory, the quilts are rounded the same way on each bed, the beds and the quilts are white. It looks like an Arab cemetery. The floor boards are wide and warped in the middle of the aisle, you see the parallel boards, the parallel beds, on the walls you see a recess here and there for a window. The floor creaks beneath your shoes. The lighted lamps hang from the ceiling. At the end of the dormitory there is a night light showing through the white cloth that covers the cubicle of the teacher supervising the dormitory. You go into the cloakroom. Dominique Vurse is sitting on the low window sill. Dominique Vurse is smoking blue Gaulois cigarettes and reading. Catherine Legrand is standing in the middle of the cloakroom. The cupboards are closed, you see the locks empty of their keys. Catherine Legrand doesn't know whose cupboards they are. There is a row of coat pegs, all but two are empty, one has a black smock, the other a dirty-looking white bathrobe. You see a chestnut tree through the window, it is motionless. You have to go through the cloakroom to get to the washroom where the washbasins are against the wall. The enamel shines in the light that falls on it from the ceiling. It is cold. It is late. Ordinarily at this time of day the lights are out the clothes hooks are full. Mother of Saint Alexander will supervise the dormitory tonight. You have permission to do whatever you like until eleven o'clock. Dominique Vurse offers Catherine Legrand a cigarette. Catherine Legrand sits beside her and looks at the title of the book Dominique Vurse is reading, it is a book that Catherine Legrand has never heard of. Véronique Legrand and Catherine Legrand will have parallel beds. When you are in bed you can hold hands with the person in the other bed. Véronique Legrand isn't in the dormitory. You left her drawing in the study room with Mother of Saint John the Baptist beside her. You leave the cloakroom to go to the washroom where you brush your teeth. Catherine Legrand is in front of the row of washbasins where the boarders wash in the morning. The walls are on the north side, the sun doesn't come in. The dormitory which you can see through the open doors is big, a person walking at the far end looks little. Suzanne Prat comes up the stairway and into the dormitory, you hear her calling Dominique Vurse from way off, you hear the wood of the floor creak beneath her hobnail boots. Suzanne Prat is in the washroom with Catherine Legrand, she starts to wash her face, you see her twist her hair, it is sticking to her neck and cheeks, black and damp. She splashes water onto the floor and onto the next washbasins. Catherine Legrand who is walking behind her gets wet. Suzanne Prat whom you have left in the washroom to go and sit beside Dominique Vurse yells for someone to throw her a towel, she has forgotten to take hers. The walls of the cloakroom and the walls of the dormitory are high bare and painted with enamel. Dominique Vurse says Catherine Legrand can borrow *La Nouvelle Héloïse* which she goes and looks for in the cupboard, you see her standing on tiptoe disarranging piles of linen and pulling out sweaters before she finds the book she is looking for. Since Suzanne Prat continues to yell for someone to bring her a towel, Dominique Vurse goes and does it. Then Catherine Legrand walks up and down the dormitory with *La Nouvelle Héloïse* under her arm. Valerie Borge's bed is next to Anne-Marie Brunet's, Catherine Legrand looks between Valerie Borge's bed and the wall, on that side Valerie Borge hasn't any neighbor. In the drawer of the low table at the head of her bed there is a handkerchief full of the perfume that Valerie Borge uses. Catherine Legrand takes Valerie Borge's folded handkerchief and puts it in the pocket of her smock. A sweet smell, but the taste is too bitter. Catherine Legrand walks up and down the dormitory. Her thoughts are pleasant and unpleasant at the same time. Whenever you walk in front of the recess of one of the walls you see Valerie Borge's bed and Anne-Marie Brunet's bed next to each other. Véronique Legrand runs through the door that leads to the stairway and into the dormitory. Mother of Saint John the Baptist is with her, she pushes her from behind and shuts the door after Véronique Legrand has entered the room. Catherine Legrand shows her where the washroom

is, walks with her, and sits on a washbasin while
Véronique Legrand brushes her teeth. In a little
while it will be dark in the dormitory. For a few
minutes you will still see the light shining through
the white cloth of the cubicle where Mother of
Saint Alexander will sleep tonight. Maybe you will
see a pocket light go back and forth along the lines
of a book under Dominique Vurse's or Suzanne Prat's
sheet while Dominique Vurse or Suzanne Prat is
careful not to make a circle of light on the ceiling.
Then you won't see anything any more because
everyone will be asleep in the dormitory, because
not a gleam will come in from the garden. It will
be dark. It is at dawn that you will see the shape
of the opoponax sitting on the window sill. I am
the opoponax. Valerie Borge you make fun of him.
No doubt it is out of fear that you don't answer
the letters that are sent to you. This very day you
will see how powerful he is and learn the price of
displeasing him. I am the opoponax. Valerie Borge
reads the opoponax letter in the handwriting which
she now knows behind her desk. Catherine Legrand
looks at the paper that Valerie Borge is reading from
across the room noticing that Anne-Marie Brunet
is busy writing in her notebook and doesn't see.
Valerie Borge brings her head out from behind the
desk when she hears a noise in the classroom. Some
pupils stand up. Marielle Balland points to the window for Valerie Borge who asks what's the matter.
Valerie Borge watches first one flame then another

pass behind the pane coming from the right side of the party wall and going across the window horizontally, Valerie Borge drops the top of her desk. The pupils nearest the window are standing up, now going forward to see what's happening now backing up when the flame appears again. Mademoiselle Doullier manages to obtain calm, manages to get each pupil to sit in her seat without talking. Mademoiselle Doullier says that there is no reason to carry on this way since the flames that you see are coming from the forge next door, that they will stop in a few minutes, that it is a phenomenon that occurs when you touch molten metal. Valerie Borge and Catherine Legrand are looking at the window. You see the flames reappear regularly, they are longer and longer and cover almost the whole surface of the window. Right now you can't tell whether the fire is coming from the forge or from the building you are in. So Mademoiselle Doullier is unable to maintain calm in the classroom. The desks are open. Some pupils are standing on their seats, others are beside the door. You hear the roar the fire makes as it passes in front of the window. Mademoiselle Doullier leads the pupils out of the classroom and into the playground. You go through the halls you go down the stairs. Mother of Saint John of God announces to the pupils that the fire has stopped and that you may begin the Latin lesson. Mother of Saint John of God says that due to the interruption caused by the pupils' panic you have lost ten minutes of the Latin lesson, Mother of Saint John of God says that it's not worth getting excited about, it is nothing but a furnace or an overheated foundry. I am the opoponax. Perhaps this warning will be sufficient for you. It depended on him alone whether you perished and the whole class along with you. Answer this letter. I am the opoponax. Catherine Legrand can see the red writing from where she is. Anne-Marie Brunet sitting next to Valerie Borge leans over to see what it is, but Valerie Borge puts the paper with the previous ones. Valerie Borge shifts around on the bench, turns around several times to glance behind her. Catherine Legrand is looking at Mother of Saint John of God. You are up to object clauses introduced by *quod*. Mother of Saint John of God says that the conjunction *quod* means therefore. The clauses it introduces express a statement of fact, therefore you put the verb in the indicative. You write the example that Mother of Saint John of God is writing on the blackboard in your notebooks, *Praetereo quod se pulchrum cogitat.* Valerie Borge leans over Anne-Marie Brunet's right shoulder to see what she wrote before the Latin sentence. Anne-Marie Brunet whispers something in her ear. Valerie Borge shakes her head no. So Anne-Marie Brunet turns away from her and won't let her see what she has written in her notebook, Valerie Borge tries to pull it from under Anne-Marie Brunet's elbow. Anne-Marie Brunet begins to protest out loud by mistake. Mother of Saint John of God looks in their direction. Anne-Marie Brunet gets all red when Mother of Saint John of God tells Valerie Borge to leave the room. Anne-Marie Brunet stands up and says, Mother it was my fault. Mother Superior comes into the classroom. Mother of Saint Jules stands up. Mother Superior walks up the center aisle while everyone stands up beside her desk. You hear a desk top slam. Nicole Marre drops a book, you see that she has caught her foot in her satchel on the floor beside her desk. Mother Superior says something to Mother of Saint Jules who nods her head yes then Mother Superior turns toward the pupils and says that Anne Gerlier Marie Démone Anne-Marie Brunet are wanted in the parlor. Mother Superior says, You may be seated. Anne Gerlier Marie Démone Anne-Marie Brunet begin putting away their things. Mother Superior and Mother of Saint Jules are talking, you can't hear what they are saying. When Mother Superior leaves everyone stands up, then Mother Superior says, You may remain seated so everyone sits down again. Marie-José Broux who is behind the others gets up after you have already sat down again, Mother of Saint Jules tells her to sit down again. Marielle Balland opens the door for Mother Superior and closes it after her. There are people coming and going in the playground, parents of pupils you don't know, women dressed in black, men in hats. Anne Gerlier Marie Démone Anne-Marie Brunet leave the classroom. Mother of Saint Jules tells Marie-José Broux that she will have to ring the bell for Anne-Marie Brunet. She doesn't know how to do it, you hear the clapper rub against the bell several times before making a clear sound. You see some pupils leaving the playground, you see them taking their smocks off as they go. The smell of pancakes comes through the open gate it is the village fair the streets are full of people going in all directions. You see herds of cows and oxen who have the same rust color going by, you see horse-drawn traps, you hear the shouts the men make to urge on the animals you see men wearing straw hats, you see men carrying rectangular wicker baskets, you see men in pleated smocks, these are the horse dealers, the animal traders who walk in groups, you recognize them by their mottled cheeks and gnarled sticks. The smell of orange blossoms, which are used to make the pancakes, spreads through the village. The bakeries have made the pancakes during the night, now the smell mingles with that of the animals. There are movements whose sounds reach the playground, bleating, mooing, the squawking of chickens tied by their feet and lying on their sides. The pupils walk around in the playground, you see them in groups by the gate, you see them going back and forth between the parlor and the playground. Valerie Borge Sophie Rieux Suzanne Prat Marie-José Broux say in loud voices that everyone should have a holiday because of the fair. Denise Causse says that it's not fair that some pupils have the day off, those whom their parents came for, that it's not right. Then you see the group get bigger, it becomes a crowd of boarders which the day pupils join after a moment. You hear loud protests, you see the fever overtake everyone, you see the pupils going from one group to another, at last columns are formed, you hear them singing songs against school. The pupils are singing with their arms around each other's shoulders. You stop singing and decide that you are agreed, you are all agreed to go on strike, that there will be no retreat. You walk through the playground shouting, making the sound of a mob, chanting We want a holiday, we're on strike. In this manner you reach the front steps. Everyone is on top of everyone else shouting and calling Mother Superior who suddenly appears and holds the balustrade with both hands. A great silence falls. You look at each other. You wait for someone to speak. Mother Superior asks for an explanation of this uproar which can be heard all over the house. Nobody speaks, then you hear murmuring in which you can distinguish the words you were just saying when you were shouting strike, holiday, fair, then all the voices rise at once. Mother Superior waits motionless for the noise to die down. When she can speak, you hear her say, Mesdemoiselles your conduct is ridiculous, you hear her say that even if her intention had been to grant everyone an afternoon's holiday there could be no question of it under the present circumstances, you hear her say that you will spend the afternoon in the study room, you hear her say that the whole school will be kept in, you hear her say that if those responsible for this rebellion do not come and identify themselves the boarders will be kept in four Sundays in a row. You see Mother Superior let go of the balustrade and go back into the house. Mother of the Infant Jesus runs out and asks Marie-José Broux to go and ring the bell. You line up in front of the steps. You see several boarders hanging their heads. Then you see Frédérique Darse go and say something to Mother of the Infant Jesus standing on the steps who nods her head yes. Frédérique Darse walks down the line whispering to day pupils in different classes. Then you see several day pupils leave the line and go with her, you see them walk up the steps, you see them walk behind Mother of the Infant Jesus to go to Mother Superior's office. You are talking about the opoponax at four-thirty play period, everyone is around Valerie Borge. Valerie Borge says that now she is afraid. Catherine Legrand laughs at her. You go over the class to see who the opoponax could be. Nicole Marre says I am the opoponax, so everyone looks at her. But nobody believes her because she bursts out laughing and begins to run holding out her arms and shouting o-po-po-nax. Mother of the Infant Jesus standing by the wall that divides the two playgrounds signals to her by waving her hand. Noémie Mazat sees Marielle Balland Sophie Rieux Laurence Bouniol Julienne Pont Marie Démone Anne Gerlier Denise Causse Anne-Marie Brunet Marguerite-Marie Le Monial Marie-José Broux Catherine Legrand around Valerie Borge. Noémie Mazat comes over to see what is going on. The panels of her smock which is torn in back flap as she walks. When she gets there you ask her who she thinks the opoponax is. Valerie Borge shows her the letters she has received. Noémie Mazat begins reading them. She is up to the third one when she looks up because you hear the sound of a ball being hit in the back of the yard. Suzanne Prat Gabrielle Murteau Nathalie Deleu have begun to play volley ball. Noémie Mazat gives the opoponax letters to Valerie Borge who catches one of them in mid-air, you see her run off toward the volley-ball net. You hear Denise Causse say, Catherine Legrand is the opoponax. Anne-Marie Brunet Valerie Borge Marielle Balland Sophie Rieux Julienne Pont Marie Démone Anne Gerlier Laurence Bouniol Marguerite-Marie Le Monial Marie-José Broux turn toward Catherine Legrand and look at her. Catherine Legrand gets all red and waves her hand no then she bursts out laughing and Valerie Borge who is looking at her says, No it's not Catherine Legrand. Marguerite-Marie Le Monial says you can torture everyone until you find out who the opoponax is. Marielle Balland Nicole Marre and someone else, maybe Denise Causse, say that that's a good idea. Valerie Borge says that in that case they must begin with Marguerite-Marie Le Monial seeing that it was her idea and that anyway it isn't mean because everyone wants to be the opoponax. Mother of the Infant Jesus comes over to the group you are with to listen to what you are saying. Valerie Borge whose body is hidden by Marielle Balland Denise Causse Anne Gerlier has time to put the opoponax letters in her pocket under her

225

handkerchief. When Mother of the Infant Jesus is close enough to hear what you are saying you pretend you were talking about the story Valerie Borge is telling. Marie-José Broux says that if she were Orphire and Rennie she would not have been so afraid, that a corpse can't hurt anyone, Marie-José Broux tells a story in which it is a man who comes out of a fireplace fully armed and firing on the people in the room with revolvers, then everyone begins to talk at once, Mother of the Infant Jesus who has her arms crossed laughs and shakes her head. You hear someone say that a man isn't scary, but a ghost is something else again, you hear someone say it isn't like the opoponax it must have been Denise Causse because everyone stops talking and gives her a dirty look but Mother of the Infant Jesus hasn't heard anything. Catherine Legrand sitting in the tree reads the note that Valerie Borge put behind the piano in the study room over and over. Valerie Borge apologizes to the opoponax for having told everybody about him, saying that she won't do it any more, that she will say that she, Valerie Borge, is the opoponax, this way nobody will think about it any more, that she hopes to keep on corresponding with him in spite of the mistake she made. Catherine Legrand makes herself comfortable with her buttocks in the fork of the tree and her legs stretched out on a large branch. You can see the sky through the oak leaves, some stand out against the cerulean blue, you can see their jagged edges. By turning her head from where she is Catherine Legrand can see the river that the tree overhangs. It is full of big stones, of trees growing between them, of young elms and poplars. The water makes a steady sound with the current and the eddies that form around the rocks. Catherine Legrand closes her eyes. In the study room Valerie Borge turns around and sees that Catherine Legrand has put her head in her arms on the table as if she were crying or as if she were sleeping. Valerie Borge tries to speak to Catherine Legrand who sees her through the space that she has left between her head and her left arm. Catherine Legrand pretends not to see her. So Valerie Borge writes something on a piece of paper. Suddenly Catherine Legrand feels an eraser thrown at her back and straightening up sees that Valerie Borge is motioning to her to pick up the note that she has thrown in the side aisle. When Catherine Legrand opens her eyes she decides she must have been asleep because the light has changed. The water which was transparent a little while ago is now the cerulean blue of the sky, the trees are ocher orange pale pink. Catherine Legrand gets down from the tree to take a book from the satchel that you left in the grass. You have to do your Latin homework for tomorrow. Catherine Legrand reads the passage from the *Georgics* slowly from beginning to end. You don't understand it, sometimes you think you recognize a word or a group of words because the root is similar to one or more French words but if you look at the notes at the bottom of the page you find that you haven't understood a thing unless they are only there to create confusion, to deceive the pupil, to give a false scent. It is obvious that you aren't going to prepare the passage, you can't do it without the dictionary without the grammar which you didn't put into your satchel on the pretext that it would be too heavy. Catherine Legrand rereads the passage that Mother of Saint John of God has assigned, picking out the two verses she understands, *Restitit, Eurydicenque suam, jam luce sub ipsa, immemor, heu! victusque animi respexit*. The assignment includes verse four hundred ninety and most of verse four hundred ninety-one. You write four hundred ninety, four hundred ninety-one, Canto Four, in your notebook. On the previous page there is a bas-relief in which you see Orpheus turning toward Eurydice and taking her hand, their heads their round cheeks look alike, their necks have the same curve as they turn toward each other, the arm of Orpheus which is in front of Eurydice's hand is curved in front of one of her breasts. You see that Eurydice is wearing a peplos, you see that Orpheus is wearing a chlamys. You will have to pay close attention in Latin class and raise your hand to be called on when you come to verse four hundred eighty-five. At first Mother of Saint John of God will pretend not to see that you are raising your finger then after several verses she will say, Catherine Legrand, will you please continue, then you will say Just a moment, *restitit*, et cetera. You won't do any school work today. You close the satchel. Catherine Legrand climbs an aspen because of its position over the river which it overhangs at an angle. The main branches are almost touching the water, they are parallel to the surface of the water and all turned toward the river because it is on this side that the tree is most developed. When you are flat on your stomach on one of them and watching the water flow after a moment you think you are moving too so you either hug the branch or you let yourself go swinging from it as if to fall into the water when you lean over you see that there isn't anything between you and it, you let your legs hang down to get a boost and fit them around the branch again, you stick them out, you hoist yourself up, you are lying flat on your stomach, watching the water go by. The leaves of the aspen have long flexible stems, maybe this is why they flutter. You see the flowers of the tree, which look as if they were made of brown plush, hanging from very short stems. You see Véronique Legrand arrive and jump from one rock to the next in the river. Suddenly she stops, you see her bend over, she is walking with little steps on the rock platform, you can't see her any more because she has gone behind a rock. You hurry down from the tree to go with Véronique Legrand, scraping your knees your thighs your legs against the bark. As you run you watch the place where Véronique Legrand disappeared, the gray stones are in the light when it rains, blue in the morning, pink in the afternoon, blue in the evening. When you catch up with Véronique Legrand you see that she is watching a snake coiling or uncoiling in an underwater cave. You see the colors of the snake. Véronique advances or retreats according to whether she thinks the snake is coming out of the water or going deeper into it. So you get a dead stick and you begin to poke in the rocky cavity inserting the stick under one of the rings so the snake will uncoil so that you can see all of him but the snake won't come out of the hole, he keeps on coiling and uncoiling.

You say, *Mon enfant ma soeur songe à la douceur d'aller là-bas vivre ensemble aimer à loisir aimer et mourir au pays qui te ressemble.* You say that there is no return when the chestnut trees have a sad smell when you see only the green of the lime trees. You say that there is no return when from the group you are in you watch the figures in the other groups. If the paths are raked, if you have put away the wheelbarrows, the pitchforks, the sweepers, if there aren't any leaves on the ground, if there aren't any flowers, if the floor of the covered playground

231

is without dust, you say that you don't see it. You say, the hour when you couldn't go out with the vertical sun the indigo sky the ultramarine sky, the white sky, the afternoon wind in the trees. The image. The hills or the banks of clouds or the rain. The journeys to rivers. The hikes in forests, the games. You say that Valerie Borge's hands legs face are a glowing brown, that Valerie Borge wears a white shirtwaist under her smock, that Valerie Borge is still wearing the woolen undershirt that you keep on all winter. You say that it is April, that the flowers are fresh on the trees or else that the flowers cover the trees. You say that it is October, that you push aside the fallen flowers with your foot. You say that you are walking and holding Véronique Legrand by the hand. You say that you are the opoponax. You say that you are running down the hill. You say that you are looking for tunes for the poems that you know. You say that you are waiting for letters from Valerie Borge. You say that you are planning to travel. To Mexico for the tiered temples. To Colorado for the orange valleys. To China for the deserts of yellow dust. To Greece for the men in fustanellas or tutus. To Persia to see girls dance in harem skirts. To the Poles because of the day and the night. Catherine Legrand and Véronique Legrand go through the main gate which is open. You hear the voices of the pupils in the yard. You walk on. The boarders have arrived. Véronique Legrand and Catherine Legrand stay side by side a moment watching. Marie

Démone and Anne Gerlier are seen in the yard with the statue. They are in a group in which you can see only them because someone else who is nearer is in the way. Véronique Legrand and Catherine Legrand walk side by side a moment, Véronique Legrand leaves Catherine Legrand and turns right toward the girls in her class who are under the covered playground. Catherine Legrand goes up to the group of boarders which Julienne Pont and Laurence Bouniol have joined. Catherine Legrand does not run. No, Valerie Borge isn't there. Yes, she will arrive any minute unless she is still on vacation for a few days. You don't know whether Valerie Borge is coming, you wonder whether Valerie Borge is coming, she is coming, you see her come through the gate, someone is walking beside her with her bags, someone goes up the front steps with her, someone kisses her and leaves. You run to meet Valerie Borge. Valerie Borge and Catherine Legrand meet in the first yard by the front steps, you jostle each other, you clap each other on the back, you hug. Valerie Borge and Catherine Legrand begin to fight. You see them rolling in the dust on top of each other, pulling each other, pushing each other, hitting each other trying to get away, Valerie Borge and Catherine Legrand are wrestling, Valerie Borge twists one of Catherine Legrand's wrists and Catherine Legrand twists her arm to make her let go. Suddenly Valerie Borge gets Catherine Legrand down and pins her to the ground by the arms. Mother of Saint John of God walks down the front steps, Mother of Saint John of God walks into the yard toward the place where Valerie Borge and Catherine Legrand are wrestling on the ground. Mother of Saint John of God looks at them you see her pause for a moment before going over to them, before going and saying to them Valerie Borge and Catherine Legrand will you please get up. You shake yourself and dust yourself off. Your hair is in your eyes. Catherine Legrand and Valerie Borge go over to a bench Valerie Borge puts her foot on it and ties her shoelace and pulls up her sock, you see her knee bone, you watch her do the same with the other leg she ties the untied shoelace and pulls up the sock. Valerie Borge takes off her coat and asks Catherine Legrand to hold it for her while she fixes her clothes, Catherine Legrand watches Valerie Borge pull down her sweater through which you can see her breasts, then Valerie Borge asks for her coat back, as she hands it to her Catherine Legrand sees that her cheeks are very red. You are sitting on the benches in the party room. Above the platform a screen has been put up onto which Mother of Saint Jules Mother of Saint Alexander Mother of Saint Ignatius of Antioch are projecting a silent film. On the bench are Nicole Marre Laurence Bouniol Marie Démone Denise Causse Julienne Pont Valerie Borge Catherine Legrand Anne Gerlier. The pictures show two young boys. You see them tell each other what they want to do. The pictures follow one another very rapidly. You see that the two boys are camping. Suddenly Valerie

Borge leans toward Catherine Legrand and whispers something in her ear. The pictures on the film are cut off at the waist. You see the tops of the bodies. After the picture is fixed it shows their whole bodies again but the subtitles are cut off you don't understand what the two boys are talking about. Catherine Legrand tells Valerie Borge that she prefers travel films. Valerie Borge says that she agrees, that she wants to go to the Rocky Mountains, that she wants to go to Peru. Now the film is broken. The lights are turned on so that Mother of Saint Ignatius of Antioch can mend it. When the light goes out again you see the picture you just saw go by again then blackness then you see the two boys lying side by side in sleeping bags. The window blinds are closed. Those on the first window of the left-hand wall are apart so you can see that it is light outside, it is windy, you see part of a chestnut tree moving. Valerie Borge begins to draw in her notebook, a dog a horse a woman. Catherine Legrand looks at Valerie Borge's notebook it's the one she writes poetry in. Catherine Legrand looks at the brown spot that Valerie Borge has above her lip. Valerie Borge leans over and tells Catherine Legrand that she is bored that she is sick of boarding school. So Catherine Legrand begins to feel bored too. The two boys are lying in the sleeping bags. It must be night again. You can see that their hair is cut crew style. The film breaks again. The lights go on. Here and there in the room the pupils stand up to look at the projector. You hear the reel of film turning uselessly, then Mother of Saint Ignatius of Antioch stops it. Nicole Marre gets up and crosses the room along the side and goes and stands behind the projector. Mother of Saint John of God sees her behind her and tells her to go back to her seat. You hear everyone begin to talk in an undertone so that Mother Superior asks you to be quiet. Nicole Marre has gone back and is standing behind Mother of Saint Ignatius of Antioch Mother of Saint Alexander and Mother of Saint John of God, after she pretended to return to her bench, you saw her sneak all the way around the room and come and stand against the door in back. The lights are put out. You hear the footsteps of Nicole Marre running back to her seat. Valerie Borge bends down to pick up the notebook that she has dropped at her feet. The white light that comes from the image projected on the screen illuminates her face, you see her hair on each side of her face. The boys are walking side by side and talking, you can tell because of the gestures they make, because there are dashes indicating dialogue in the subtitles below the pictures. You see them begin to run. They gather wood which they drag back behind them and put in a pile. Next you see them make a fire. Valerie Borge tells Catherine Legrand that she is going to show her a poem that she wrote last year. Catherine Legrand turns toward Valerie Borge on the bench while she looks for the poem in the notebook while she stops at one page while she goes on to the following page. Valerie Borge hands the open notebook to Catherine

Legrand pointing to the poem on the left-hand page. Catherine Legrand holds the notebook up to her eyes. It is hard to make out the writing by the light of the image projected on the screen. Catherine Legrand reads, Like a melancholy snake the frost flees from the field, its silver body gleams imprisoned in the cold. All at once Valerie Borge grabs Catherine Legrand's arm and squeezes it. Catherine Legrand lifts her head and looks at the screen. You see that the two boys have the barrels of guns aimed at their chests you see them fall because the gunmen must have fired although you didn't hear the report. The subtitle indicates that they fell crying Long live Christ the King. Then Valerie Borge takes Catherine Legrand's hand in hers but then you see the boys lying side by side in the sleeping bags which means that they are dreaming. You are walking through the acacia path with baskets full of petals. You are preparing the way for the procession. You have red tulips red peonies red roses, you have lilies white tulips white peonies white roses arum lilies. You are making designs on the ground with the flower petals according to Mother of Saint Nicholas' plan. Some of them are still whole, you have to tear off the petals before laying them on the ground. Nicole Marre Valerie Borge Laurence Bouniol Marie-José Broux Catherine Legrand are on the path. You are squatting with your hands full of petals. After a while the baskets are empty. You go into the flowerbeds to fill them with new flowers which you pick. Mother of Saint Nicholas says that first you must take the flowers in fullest bloom. Some have even dropped part of their blossoms on the ground, you take the fallen petals too. It takes time to fill the baskets. Mother of Saint Nicholas clears leaves dirty flowers and bits of wood and paper from the paths still to be lined, then she rakes them. You must also prepare the place where the procession will stop, here you set up altars which you will cover with petals and on which you will put vases of cut flowers tomorrow morning. From way off, from the meadow, from the front steps, from the wall dividing the two playgrounds, you can see the altars under their white cloths with the empty vases that you have already put in place. Mother of Saint Nicholas' designs are arranged at the sides of the path to leave room to walk. There are places where the design covers the whole width of the path so that you will walk right on the flowers here. You make a puzzle with the petals, arranging first the red ones then the white ones in the spaces left free. You have no more petals in the baskets. You go back to pick the flowers in the flower-beds. There are also the low rosebushes, the climbing rose bushes, those that are against the walls, those that form arches over the paths. You have stools, you have stepladders. Nicole Marre goes everywhere with a stepladder which she has slung over her shoulder and which she keeps putting down at her feet because it is heavy, sometimes she can't hold onto it and you hear it fall down. Nicole Marre puts the ladder against the receding façade opposite the Carmelites' garden.

You see her go up the rungs with the basket over her arm. Nicole Marre begins to pick the highest roses so that she is about to lose her balance any moment. The basket which she has propped against one of the rungs falls. You see the splashes of red at the foot of the ladder. Nicole Marre begins to pick up the petals one at a time she puts them back into the basket with bits of dirt. Nicole Marr decides to move the ladder, she walks toward the arches of the iris path. As she passes her Mother of Saint Nicholas sees that there are red and white flowers in the same basket. Mother of Saint Nicholas says, But I told you not to mix the colors, so Nicole Marre comes down from the ladder and begins sorting the flowers and petals, leaving the more numerous red ones in the basket and making a pile of the white ones which she puts on the ground. Valerie Borge and Catherine Legrand are picking flowers in the flowerbeds behind the thuja hedge. There haven't been any open flowers for a long time so you pick all the flowers indiscriminately, you take them barely open, some are damp, you pick buds and throw them helter-skelter into the baskets. You take the flowers all the flowers, you will take the petals off sitting on the ground, you will tear the petals you won't be able to separate those of the buds which are still stuck together, the baskets are full of tulips peonies lilies roses. Valerie Borge and Catherine Legrand are rehearsing the procession, when the priest stops, how children throw flowers on the monstrances, Valerie Borge and Catherine Legrand both receive the red flowers on their foreheads in their hair on their cheeks down their necks. Valerie Borge and Catherine Legrand are surrounded by red flowers. You think. You don't know. You say that there is no point offering your soul to the devil the devil doesn't want it according to what you have heard on the subject. You say that he doesn't come at midnight when you summon him. You say that he doesn't come with an infernal smell that he doesn't jump into the chalk circle that he doesn't appear in a sulphurous and fuliginous light that you don't see him suddenly take shape beginning with the head or with the feet or with the middle of the body like the Cheshire cat. You say that the window is open, that you see something moving in the meadow, it must be the grass, you see the spots made by the daisies, you hear the hooting of an owl. You say that you are at Marie Démone's house, that Mother of Saint John of God Marielle Balland Laurence Bouniol Nicole Marre Sophie Rieux Anne Gerlier Denise Causse Anne-Marie Brunet Marie-José Broux Marguerite-Marie Le Monial Valerie Borge Catherine Legrand are there. You say that you are sitting on straight chairs and armchairs. You say that Valerie Borge and Catherine Legrand are sitting in the same armchair because there is one seat too few, you say that you are having tea, you say that your hands shake when you hold the teacup. You say that you are walking in the country-side, you say that the low hills form a circle, that the villages look smaller and smaller, you say that the sky is pale blue, that Catherine Legrand and Valerie Borge are walking hand in hand. You say that Valerie Borge lets go of Catherine Legrand's hand and begins to run, that Catherine Legrand can't catch her, that Valerie Borge falls down in the grass, you say that Catherine Legrand who is running after her trips and falls too, on top of Valerie Borge. You say that the ground smells, you say that the grass is cut, that you see a field-mouse hole, you say that Valerie Borge makes a cricket come out of a tiny hole by sticking a twig into it, you say that you come back in the evening in a covered truck that it is cold because of the air that whistles by that you have blankets over you that Valerie Borge and Catherine Legrand have the same blanket over them under which they are holding hands. You say that it is dark that Catherine Legrand lies down in the damp grass that she stays there looking at the stars. You say that you are on the stage that you are having a rehearsal. You say that Mother of Saint Hippolytus has chosen a passage from the *Odyssey*, that it is Ulysses' arrival in Ithaca. You say that Catherine Legrand is the narrator, that Valerie Borge is Penelope, that Ulysses is one of the older girls Frédérique Darse whose height shoulders leonine head you admire. You say that Eumaeus is played by Gabrielle Murteau, that Suzanne Prat Nathalie Deleu Anne Gerlier are suitors. You say that Telemachus is Paule Falou the girl who reads Virgil at sight, the girl who has green eyes and a Greek nose. You say that you hear the music ordered by Ulysses after the killing he has done. You say that Catherine Legrand waits for Valerie Borge in the wings that she meets her that she kisses her on the cheek. You say that because of the music you don't notice the blood on the chairs or the brains sticking to the wood of the tables. Mother of Saint Hippolytus says that this is the principal action of the *Odyssey* because except for Telemachus' contest with Penelope's suitors, except when he leaves at the news, everything you know about the characters about Ulysses about the Trojan war the wanderings the vicissitudes, is told by people sitting around dinner tables, in Book Three Nestor to Telemachus, in Book Four Menelaus to Telemachus, in Book Eight Demodocos to those at the feast of Alcinous, in Books Nine Ten Eleven Twelve Thirteen Ulysses to Alcinous. Mother of Saint Hippolytus says that besides Menelaus tells what Proteus told him, Ulysses tells what Circe, Tiresias, Autolycos, and Agamemnon told him, Mother of Saint Hippolytus says that therefore it is the main action of the Odyssey that will be represented on the stage. You say that Valerie Borge's legs are hidden by the peplos, that she moistens her lips to make them shine, that the narrator standing at the side of the stage says, He says, looking at Penelope's lips. You say that you are rehearsing. You say that you see Valerie Borge come up to Frédérique Darse and throw her arms around her neck. You say that Valerie Borge and Catherine Legrand are hidden by the aucuba shrubs by the catacombs. You say that between the leaves you see pupils go by running walking talking eating their sandwiches, that you can see them without being seen, that on the other side of the hedge formed by the aucubas Anne-Marie Brunet and Denise Causse are sitting on the boxes, that you don't listen to what they are saying, that you are talking in low voices. You say that Valerie Borge is talking about last vacation about next vacation, Valerie Borge is talking about the carbine her father gave her, about hunting, Valerie Borge tells that once she fired a loaded Mauser rifle that you can feel the gun's recoil in your shoulder when the shot is fired, Valerie Borge is talking about friends she has, about the time when she will be out of school. You say that Catherine Legrand says to Valerie Borge, You don't love me. You say that Valerie Borge turns her head away, that she sits still leaning against the leaves of the aucuba for a moment, that when she looks at Catherine Legrand you see that she is crying, that you stand up then, you say to Valerie Borge, come, that you go into the garden in the rain, you say that Valerie Borge isn't crying, you say that Catherine Legrand doesn't give her her handkerchief because she doesn't have one. You say that Valerie Borge puts three carbine five five bullets into Catherine Legrand's hand and tells her to keep them. You say that you see the rain touching the trees, falling in front of the trunks, running off the leaves, that you make holes in the dirt of the paths when you walk, that your hair is getting wet and sticking to your face, that you are going to the end of the park. You say that there are puddles in the low places on the paths, that the rain is coming down hard, that you can't open your eyes all the way that you are keeping them half closed, you can't see ten yards in front of you anyway, it is like a fog that the wind pushes this way and that, that you are walking without holding hands. You say that when you are sitting on the benches again you feel your clothes sticking to your skin, that your feet are wet. You say that it is raining around the car in the back end of which Catherine Legrand and Véronique Legrand are sitting, that you aren't talking, that your head is leaning against the seat. The pavement gleams in the places where the road is curved. The ruts are full of water which the wheels of the car splash as it goes by and which sprays as high as the windows. Sometimes you sit up to look at something, then you sit back against the seat again. You can't take your mind off the sound made by the windshield wiper. There isn't anyone on the roads. The villages you go through have closed doors, closed windows some of which have lights in them. You see that the fields are flooded. The water comes up above the ground between the blades of grass. You say that if you were walking you would sink in. You see the water sliding along the electric wires, dropping off the trees, sometimes you see a bird sitting still. The leaves of the trees seem curled because of the water, so that you can't tell what species they belong to any more. You say, *Les soleils mouillés de*

244

ces ciels brouillés pour mon esprit ont les charmes si mystérieux de tes traîtres yeux brillant à travers leurs larmes. At the bend in the road you see the cathedral. The rain makes a screen between it and the car which is going toward it. From now on you won't lose sight of it again except for a moment when you go into a little valley, then you will see it reappear through the rain. Suddenly you will see a ray of sunlight cut through the clouds making the falling water shine, then the cathedral will also begin to shine from afar under the water and the sunlight. You are going to Rivajou with Mother of Saint Jules. There are Marie-José Broux Marielle Balland Sophie Rieux Nicole Marre Marguerite-Marie Le Monial Anne-Marie Brunet Laurence Bouniol Julienne Pont Marie Démone Anne Gerlier Denise Causse Valerie Borge Catherine Legrand. On the platform of the train station you watch the pantograph of a locomotive fold and unfold as it rubs the wires. The train that you take is a steam engine. It stops alongside the platform with a long braking. Valerie Borge and Catherine Legrand are at the window leaning out as far as they can. Catherine Legrand has Valerie Borge's hair in her face. Catherine Legrand sees Valerie Borge in profile with her hair lifted, she sees the descending arch of the left eyebrow the temple the cheekbone the cheek the line of the jaw the neck Valerie Borge's hands are resting on the lowered windowpane. The wind blows the steam down all along the train, at times you can't see each other any more, then you throw back your head and rub your eyes. Mother of Saint Jules is in the next compartment with Marielle Balland Nicole Marre Laurence Bouniol Julienne Pont Marie Démone Anne Gerlier Denise Causse Anne-Marie Brunet Marguerite-Marie Le Monial Marie-José Broux Sophie Rieux. Valerie Borge tells Catherine Legrand that the train will not stop, that it will keep on going all day and all night, that tomorrow it will keep on going and tomorrow night and so on forever. You laugh at this train that won't stop. You say, *Des meubles luisants polis par les ans décoreraient notre chambre les plus rares fleurs mêlant leurs odeurs aux vagues senteurs de l'ambre, les riches plafonds les miroirs profonds la splendeur orientale tout y parlerait à l'âme en secret sa douce langue natale.* The train stops at Rivajou. Mother of Saint Jules is standing in front of the glass of the compartment Valerie Borge and Catherine Legrand are in, Mother of Saint Jules is waiting for them to come out. You are walking through the water. You have on short panties so you can cross the river in certain places. You ford it. On the other side there is a wood, rocks. This is where you eat sitting on stones. You run over the rocks jumping from one to the next. You run races which Valerie Borge wins. Nicole Marre pretends to fall off a rock and really does fall so that everyone yells and runs toward her. But she hasn't hurt herself. You walk through the water. You try to catch fish by putting your hand under the stones. Valerie Borge catches two. They are gudgeon. You watch them move in the grass. You put them back in the water after a moment. Valerie Borge catches something which she takes out from behind a big stone, it is a snake which she is holding by the head. Sophie Rieux beside her begins to scream and tries to run out of the water, so that she twists her ankle against a root, she is sitting beside the water holding the ankle and saying that it hurts, Valerie Borge goes over to her with the snake in her hand. Sophie Rieux limps away so Valerie Borge lets the snake go. Mother of Saint Jules says that Sophie Rieux has sprained her ankle because she can't step on it, Mother of Saint Jules says that the ankle will swell. You climb the trees that are beside the river. You go along the branches holding onto them with your arms and legs until you reach the end and the branch bends, then you drop down to the ground. Julienne Pont tries to get down from the tree which she is very high up in upside down, that is, with her head down. You see her hanging from a branch by her knees, her hands are holding the branch below, her hair is hanging in front of it, you see her open her knees and fall, as she goes around the branch she is holding onto she says that she is doing a somersault, the weight of her body almost makes her let go and she hurts her back this is why she is sitting in a fork without moving leaning against the trunk of the tree. You practice jumping from one tree to another over the rocks. Valerie Borge looks at the tree into which she is about to jump and whose branches are touching the one you are in. Then

Catherine Legrand jumps first with a shout, and now that she has jumped she can't stop going from one tree to the other. Valerie Borge jumps shouting behind her to catch her. Valerie Borge and Catherine Legrand are sitting side by side on a big branch. Catherine Legrand asks Valerie Borge if they are going into the cave which you can see and into which Mother of Saint Jules has forbidden them to go, Valerie Borge says they will, that they must take sticks to feel their way because they don't have a light. You go swimming. The water is like spring water, ice-cold on your stomach then on your chest and now around your neck and shoulders when you swim. Léon Torpusse holds back the branches of the hedge so Catherine Legrand can go by. Catherine Legrand enters the hole in the hedge and the spines of the blackthorns and blackberries which Léon Torpusse lets go of just as she goes by land in her face. Catherine Legrand has cuts on her face her legs her thighs. Léon Torpusse is sitting on his heels. Léon Torpusse laughs very loud and pounds the ground with his fists. Pierre Doumieux is standing behind him. He isn't laughing. Catherine Legrand rushes toward Léon Torpusse who jumps to his feet and begins running, Catherine Legrand runs after Léon Torpusse. Pierre Doumieux runs behind Catherine Legrand. Léon Torpusse grabs the lowest branch of a tree as he runs, you can see his body swing back and forth with the momentum. Catherine Legrand hits him on the thighs on the legs, Léon Torpusse tries to pull himself up into the tree by sticking his legs out. Catherine Legrand gets hold of his foot, then his calf and pulls with all her might until Léon Torpusse lets go of the branch and falls on his back. Then Catherine Legrand jumps onto his stomach and thighs and hits his face. Pierre Doumieux tells them to stop fighting pushing Catherine Legrand who falls on her behind, forcing Léon Torpusse and Catherine Legrand to stand up. You are retracing your steps along the meadow. You are going to look for Véronique Legrand and Jeanne Doumieux. Pierre Doumieux Jeanne Doumieux Catherine Legrand Véronique Legrand Léon Torpusse are going with the hunters to flush quail and partridge in the tablelands. You are on the rock-covered hills. The sky is pale. The earth and the hills are the same ocher color. The dry vegetation blends with the rocky soil. It consists of whitish lichens, thorny junipers and sumac. You walk ahead of the hunters. You take the place of the dogs. You flush the birds which you can't see from a distance. You see them at your feet just as they fly away. You think they are rocks that suddenly rise but you hear the sound of their wings beating. Behind, the hunters fire before the birds have gained altitude. They are in a row. Jeanne Doumieux Véronique Legrand Pierre Doumieux Catherine Legrand Léon Torpusse walk in a row in front of them. From time to time a snake moves away from a stone which you are about to step on but at this time of the year they are slow, they say it is because they have no venom. You walk. The

249

tablelands go on and on with little valleys and gentle depressions, you can't see the end of them. You walk. You meet a shepherd following his sheep. He drives them ahead of him to keep them from blocking your path. He hits some of them with his stick and shouts. Ahead of him a yellow dog jumps, barks, catches the sheep by the wool and the legs, goes ahead of them and jumps at their throats. The sheep are crowded together, and bleat in unison. You hear the bells they have at their necks which are jiggled by their trotting their frolicking and their swerving in front of the dog. You see the sheep bump into each other, you see one get up onto another's back and fall off again, now they are running in front of the hunters in front of Jeanne Doumieux Véronique Legrand Pierre Doumieux Catherine Legrand Léon Torpusse. You wait for them to pass, the shepherd runs after them shouting *Puta de miladiou de macarelle de bondiou* and other oaths that you don't understand. You walk away from the hunters. One of them tells Léon Torpusse to go back to the house. Léon Torpusse says something you can't hear, then the hunter runs after him and hits him on the back of the head, Léon Torpusse puts up his arm to protect himself but the hunter takes the arm away and hits him again and tells him to scram. Then Léon Torpusse begins to run. Véronique Legrand Jeanne Doumieux Catherine Legrand Pierre Doumieux run behind him. After a while you sit down on the ground, you watch the hunters getting farther away you see their guns beside their heads, they get smaller and smaller you see them disappear behind a hill. You walk. You are going to look for medlar nuts. You hear the spring of the farm to which you are going. You make a detour around the back because you are afraid to be seen. You see the field that surrounds the farm and the wall of one side of the house, you breathe in the smell of burning leaves. You go to the second field which is separated from the first by a hedge growing out of some stones laid on top of each other without cement. As Jeanne Doumieux goes through the hole in the hedge she stubs her toe on a rock, you hear the rock slide that she starts, you sit behind the hedge, nobody comes, then you begin to gather medlars which you crack in your fingers, when you get tired of medlars you go on to walnuts, you shake the branches because you don't have any poles, a few nuts fall, you put them in your pockets. Léon Torpusse fills his beret. You climb the tree to shake the branches harder than down below where you must stand on tiptoe and can't reach them. Then you see the fat woman coming out the door of the farmhouse shouting at the top of her lungs Dirty thieves, get the hell out of there. But you don't get the hell out you keep on shaking the branches of the walnut trees. The fat woman shouts louder and louder, she keeps shouting the same thing, at last she goes to the stable, comes out with a pitchfork, comes toward you holding the pitchfork in front of her, you see her bosom heave because she is going as fast as she can but she can't run, you see her belly her buttocks then you scramble down from the tree and run away. You say that you are in the playground after the storm. You say that behind the windows of the catacombs you saw flashes of lightning cross the sky, there were several parallel streaks, you say that the trees appeared in flashes and that the rain began to fall. You say that the water is falling everywhere in the yard, in the garden, that there are ditches where there are new streams, you say that you jump over them yelling, that the air is cold and damp, that the ground and the leaves smell you say that the acacia path is a river whose water comes up to your ankles. You say that you are going into the yard to watch the water everywhere, the wet trunks, that you get up on the benches because your feet are soaking wet in your shoes, that you throw into the ditches sticks which are carried along which turn around in circles which end up getting stuck in the ground, you say *Vois sur ces canaux, courir ces vaisseaux dont l'humeur est vagabonde c'est pour assouvir ton moindre désir qu'ils viennent du bout du monde.* You say that Valerie Borge is standing on the hills that you can hear rivers flow, you say that there are sheep moving, that the clouds are dappled, you say that the sun is white, you say that the sky is pale blue, you say that you see Valerie Borge with her hair back, standing on the hills, you say that you see her small as from a distance as you approach, you say that you see the skin of her face magnified as when you are looking from very near, you say that you see Valerie Borge

standing on the hills as if you were lying on the
ground. You say that Valerie Borge is standing on
the hills, that you see her that you are looking at her,
that you hear the water of the rivers flowing, that
you hear the sheep bells, that you are looking at her.
Mademoiselle Caylus is dead. Mother Superior says
during study period that you will go to watch by her.
Valerie Borge and Catherine Legrand are in Mademoiselle Caylus' room. Mother of Saint Jules pushes
them over to the bed. You bend down to kiss the
corpse. You feel her forehead or cheek beneath your
lips. You straighten up again. You go and stand on
either side of the bed. Mother of St. Jules leaves. The
shutters are closed. There are candles. You have ro-
saries in your hands but you don't use them. You can't
take your eyes off Mademoiselle Caylus. The high
table with holy water and candles is by her head.
Mademoiselle Caylus has her hands on her chest over
the sheet. Her hair is fixed in the bun she always
wears. You see that her eyes are closed behind the
glasses. You wonder if it is true that she is dead. Her
cheeks are yellow. Valerie Borge and Catherine Legrand don't dare whisper. Suddenly you think the
corpse moves. Valerie Borge stands up and goes
toward the door. Catherine Legrand gets up too. But
it is only the jaws opening, you see the lips opening
little by little. Valerie Borge and Catherine Legrand
standing at the foot of the bed don't hold hands,
they look at Mademoiselle Caylus and wait for her
to begin to speak, for her to raise her hands and move

them in their direction. The corpse becomes motionless again. Catherine Legrand and Valerie Borge sit down beside the bed again. The thin lips are lifted at one corner of the mouth, revealing a piece of tooth, which gives Mademoiselle Caylus a peculiar smile. You go by bus to Fougerolles where Mademoiselle Caylus will be buried. The hearse is in front. You sleep against the seat because the light is gone, because you got up early. When you open your eyes you see forms go by behind the windowpanes, you see the back of the man driving the bus. Mother of Saint Jules is sitting behind him. Valerie Borge sleeps beside Catherine Legrand. Her head is bent, her hair is spread around her, you see that her mouth is half parted you see the lips over the teeth. At a bump Valerie Borge wakes with a start and sits up on the seat looking at Catherine Legrand beside her smiling at her letting her head roll onto the shoulder of Catherine Legrand who takes her hands and settles her against herself. Valerie Borge goes back to sleep. You yawn from time to time. You see that it is light, that you are crossing some mountains. At a turn in the road you see a grove of birch trees whose heads are tossing. It is cold. Marie Démone gets up and walks up the center aisle. She must be telling Mother of Saint Jules that she has a pain in her heart because you see Mother of Saint Jules give her peppermint oil on a lump of sugar and take off her cape and put it around Marie Démone and make her sit down beside her. Everyone is waking up in the bus. Sophie Rieux picks up her scarf and

puts it around her neck. Nicole Marre yells and tickles
Laurence Bouniol to wake her up. Sophie Rieux
stretches. Valerie Borge pretends to be asleep, with
her head on Catherine Legrand's shoulder. When
Catherine Legrand holds her away from her she sees
her open her eyes, smile and close her eyes again.
Catherine Legrand feels Valerie Borge squeeze her
hands. Anne-Marie Brunet stands in the aisle combing her hair. Mother of Saint Jules goes by with a
thermos, Mother of Saint Jules pours the scalding-hot
coffee into mugs, the smell of coffee spreads, you
hear the mugs and spoons clink together, Mother of
Saint Jules almost falls down because the road turns,
Julienne Pont takes the thermos from her, Mother of
Saint Jules tells her to have some coffee. Valerie Borge
sits up, she runs her hand through her hair and asks
someone to lend her a comb. It has snowed in the
mountains. You hear the wind in the trees and against
the metal of the bus. Valerie Borge and Catherine Legrand lean together again when they have finished
drinking the coffee. Valerie Borge and Catherine Legrand don't talk. Everyone around them is talking
loudly. Nicole Marre is in the aisle, she bumps into
Laurence Bouniol who yells You hurt me and Denise
Causse on whom she falls, then Denise Causse pushes
Nicole Marre off her lap and onto the floor. Mother
of Saint Jules tells her to get up and go back to her
seat. You hear pupils joking about Mademoiselle
Caylus' funeral. Marie-José Broux laughs and says
that you are going to divide up what Mademoiselle

Caylus left. Marguerite-Marie Le Monial says that she wants her false teeth. Marielle Balland says that she wants her cane. Mother of Saint Jules tells them to be quiet. You hear the mass for the dead in the church at Fougerolles. The walls the pillars the benches everything feels cold as ice. You shiver. The mass is sung by the townspeople. You shiver in the cemetery. There is water in the bottom of the grave, you see the coffin being lowered into it and hear it land with a splash. Then Marielle Balland Marguerite-Marie Le Monial Anne-Marie Brunet Denise Causse Marie-José Broux begin to cry. The cemetery is uncared for, the tombs are covered with grass with daisies with poppies. There are poppies all over the cemetery, you can see their faded blossoms bend in the wind. You see wooden crosses not one of which seems vertical, they have been pulled out of the ground, some are at angles, some have fallen across their mounds where you can just make out a tomb. There aren't any inscriptions on the mounds, there aren't any names. Melted snow is falling. You are sinking into the mud. The poppies are wet. You are standing, you are shaking hands with Mademoiselle Caylus' relatives. You say, *Les soleils couchants revêtent les champs les canaux la ville entière d'hyacinthe et d'or le monde s'endort dans une chaude lumière.* You say, *Tant je l'aimais qu'en elle encore je vis.*